B

CW01022029

Deleted

5/05

Living Proof

Living Proof

An Autobiography

Hank Williams, Jr.
with Michael Bane

G. P. Putnam's Sons
New York

Library of Congress Cataloging in Publication Data

Williams, Hank.
    Living proof.

    1. Williams, Hank. 2. Country musicians—United States Biography. I. Bane, Michael, joint author. II. Title.
ML420.W55A3   784'.092'4[B]   79-11741

ISBN 0-399-12369-5

Printed in the United States of America

CONTENTS

Living Proof

1

A Funeral in the South

They came to Montgomery by the tens of thousands—some say by the hundreds of thousands—when they buried Daddy, and no one could remember such an outpouring of grief for any one person in the South since the end of the Civil War. Hank was dead. No last names were necessary, as a local newspaper columnist in Montgomery pointed out. When you said "Hank" south of the Mason-Dixon line, there was never any doubt that you were talking about Hank Williams.

Hank was dead, and with him died, I think, a tiny portion of the South's consciousness. There is a quote of Daddy's that a lot of people have picked up on, and I think that quote ought to be carved in marble over the door of every record company in Nashville.

Daddy said, "When a hillbilly sings a crazy song, he feels crazy. When he sings 'I Laid My Mother Away,' he sees her a-laying right there in the coffin. . . . What he is singing is the hopes and prayers and dreams of what some call the common people . . . "

" . . . Of what some call the common people. . . ." There was a song, written in the mid-1960s by a couple of Nashville songwriters named John Hurley and Ronnie Wilkins, called "The Love of the Common People," and it talked about "living in the love of the common people, right from the heart of the family man." And that's what Daddy did. He was adored because no matter how big he got, no matter how many millions of records or how much money he made, he was living in the love of the common people, and he never forgot it. Not for one second.

I remember once I was sitting in a hotel room in the Jefferson Davis Hotel in Montgomery—I think the movie *Your Cheatin' Heart* was premiering then, so I must have been around sixteen years old. I was sitting up there trying to write a song, and I'd called room service for a Coke. This old black man brought the Coke up to my room, and when he came in I stopped writing to talk for a couple of minutes.

He just stood there looking at me, and then he said, "Yessir, I used to bring your father some drinks up here to his room. Yes suh, I sure do remember Mr. Hank."

And his eyes were all lit up and even though he was smiling I knew he was going to break down crying right there.

"I'm working on a song right now," I said, a little awkwardly. I was a little shaken myself.

The old man said, "Boy, am I so glad to meet you, Little Hank. I sure remember Mr. Hank. We sure all loved him."

And he left, and I swear there were tears in his eyes.

And my father loved the little people the same way, from the very depths of his being. He could be in a room with the biggest executives in the music business, and he'd wander off to go talk to the doorman or the bellboy or the maid. They were his people, and I think more than anything else, he wanted to be with them. Alabama was his home, and those "hillbillies"—he hated that word when it came from a yankee, 'cause it wasn't meant any different than "nigger"—were his root people. He didn't really want to screw around with all those other things.

10

He respected his audience as well as loved them. It was always a one-to-one basis, and that's important. You might be able to trick the public for a little while, but pretty soon they're going to figure out that you don't give a shit about them.

But not Hank.

Like he'd go out on stage and just tell the audience, big as you please, and just *talk* to them, like they were sitting around the living room of his house. "I wrote this song with so-and-so in mind and I'm feeling a little rough tonight. I've had a rough past few weeks, and my love life isn't what it's supposed to be, and I'm sure you're all the same way. . . ."

Think of it: A man saying that and then cutting into "I Can't Help It If I'm Still in Love with You," what's an audience going to do? I'll tell you: They went berserk. He would tell them the truth, and they loved him for it.

And then he was dead, and the people he loved came to pay their last respect. Red Foley sang "Peace in the Valley"; Ernest Tubb sang "Beyond the Sunset"; Roy Acuff sang "I saw the Light," Daddy's favorite hymn and maybe one of his best-known songs. Mother sat in the front row with Daddy's *second* wife, Billie Jean, but there was never any doubt as to who would become the Widow Williams. At least, I don't think Mother had any doubt at that point. She had me, Randall Hank Williams–Hank Williams Junior—and that was claim enough. Within a few weeks, Billie Jean had been pushed totally into the background. Mother had the Hank Williams' house in Nashville and, temporarily, all the royalties from Daddy's songs. I don't think I'll ever really know what happened at the funeral—Billie Jean has claimed, in print, that it was ugly; that there was a fistfight between her and Mother. Maybe that's a little far-fetched. Maybe not.

They laid my father to rest in the Oakwood Cemetery Annex, and standing next to his grave, if you listened closely, you could hear the clanking of trains and once in a while hear their lonesome whistles blow. To get to the grave, you go down a road with seven bridges, and someone wrote a song about that:

Sometimes there is a part of me
Has to turn away and go
Running like a child beneath warm stars
Down the seven bridge's road . . .

There were songs about Hank in Heaven, meeting Hank in the bye-and-bye, Hank's ghost, Hank's soul—Hank dead was bigger than Hank alive. Hank alive was still just a hillbilly singer—Hank dead was a myth, the Legend of Hank Williams.

This is where I come in, really, because I became a part of that legend. I grew up surrounded by the myth, and I accepted my place in it.

What else could I do?

There were thousands of letters to Mother and the family, expressing their personal grief at the passing of Hank Williams. The grief was almost like a living, breathing thing. Something vital had been wrested from the everyday lives of people, and they struggled to put it into words.

You're thinking that it's always that way with popular idols, and you're thinking about people like John Kennedy, or maybe Elvis Presley, and maybe to a certain extent it is.

But what surrounded the life (and, ultimately, the death) of my father goes beyond the whole concept of "fans" and "entertainers." He gave voice to people who had traditionally been ignored—even despised—the lower-class southern white; the poor farmer, the wage earner, the workingman, the God-fearing family man, the bellhop, the black field worker. What Hank Williams was saying was something they were hearing for the very first time—that they were important enough to have somebody write the soundtrack to their lives. It's a heck of a thought even now. You don't have to apologize for who or what you are; when you cry in your beer or go out raisin' hell or get down on knees in a little country church, why, that's just as important as whatever the rich folks in New York City do—maybe more important. Hank Williams' very success was like saying to a whole class of people that, see, they were so important that one of their own could go out and make a fortune by just singing about their lives.

He was a lightning rod for their hopes and dreams and their little successes and their little failures, and when he died young and forlorn, they understood, and they told the story of Hank Williams to their children. And, as in all good legends, Hank had a loving wife—no matter that he had *another* wife in between—and a son to carry on in his name. To his people, maybe he was always a legend; his music forgave them their excesses, reminded them of their good times, and never forgot that Heaven was waiting in the wings.

How could he be anything but a legend?

But legend is a funny thing. It's not real like a rock is real, or like a gun is real, but it's got the power to destroy you just as dead as a rock or a gun. It's elusive, though, just when you're ready to rear up on your hind legs and give it a fight to the finish, it slips away, and you're left struggling with a couple of armfuls of air. You can't deny it's there, but when you try to explain it, people act like you're talking about ghosts, or you're just out of your mind or something.

I'm sensitive to that, because my life was built on the legend of Hank Williams, and I know what it's like to feel it pulling until you want to scream that you're being pulled apart, but the right words never seem to come.

It's strange, but my father was fascinated with guns, and that's a fascination I inherited. Maybe his fascination was rooted in the idea that even the guns couldn't destroy the demons that were tormenting him, or maybe it's nothing so metaphysical. All I know is that guns are machines: You pull the trigger, the sear moves, causing the hammer to fall, which strikes the primer, causing an explosion. The explosion sets off the powder, and the bullet is hurled out the barrel. It's all a mechanical process, as sure as the sun rising tomorrow morning. And I never cease to marvel at that simple cause and effect, how each little part of the machine works together to create the desired end. If you're a good shot—and I am a very good

13

shot—you can make the bullet go where you want it, whether that's into a paper target or a Cape Buffalo in Africa.

I know when I pull the trigger what's going to happen, and, more importantly, I know *why* it's going to happen. And when I pull the trigger, I take full responsibility for the flight of that bullet. If there are consequences, I take them. If there is meat, I claim it. Good or bad, it's an action that I caused to happen, and I am solely responsible for the results.

It's not like life at all.

2

Montana Song

A long time before the white man came to run his cattle and build his cities, the Indians knew there was magic in the mountains. It's a magic of belonging, like you can reach out and touch the wind that howls up from the Idaho side of the Continental Divide. It's a feeling that comes over you when you pause on the trail and let the sounds of the high forest wash away the last of the city's grit—the city yells and screams and demands attention, but the forest only hints. There's a hint of running water from the valley below, barely covering a hint of sound that might be the bellow of a bull moose. Just on the edge of your perception there's the war cry of a Blackfoot warrior, the first human occupants of this land, almost lost in the ghost wind that moves the century-old trees and never lets you forget that even the rocks will one day be forgotten.

The gift of the mountains is that, if you're lucky, you become a part of the mountains, no different from the rocks or the trees or the moose that bellows in the valley. You belong, and when you belong, you begin to heal.

I blink and catch my friend and hiking companion Dick Willey staring at me.

"Maybe we'd better sit down and take a few minutes' rest," he says, taking off his field glasses and surveying the surrounding peaks. "The heck—you can't run around these mountains all day without taking a rest."

I plop down on a boulder and laugh—Dick knows what he's talking about. We're moving along the knife edge of the Continental Divide, balanced between Idaho and Montana, and at 11,000 feet the air gets thin. *Mighty* thin, especially if two short days ago you were running around Nashville like a chicken with its head cut off trying to get a flight out west.

It was so frustrating I would have screamed if it'd done any good, but I don't think even that would've worked. The harder I tried to get to Montana, the more things conspired to keep me in Nashville. Northwest Airlines was on strike, and they were one of a grand total of two airlines that flew into Missoula, where I needed to go. There were no seats available out of Nashville, or Atlanta, or even Dallas–Fort Worth, and no airline could come up with a route that would get me anywhere near Missoula in this century.

"It's fate," my business manager kept telling me. "Someone upstairs just doesn't want you to go to Montana. Forget it, and get ready for your next tour."

But I couldn't forget it any more than I could forget that next tour. I had to get to Montana, or maybe there wouldn't *be* a next tour. What I'd told everybody was that I had to go to Montana to get in shape for a hunt—like my daddy before me, I'm a hunter, and we'd been making big plans for a hunt in Canada's Northwest Territory. That country's rugged, and you don't just waltz out of the Grand Ole Opry into the Mackenzie Mountains without a lot of preparation. If I was going to hunt the Northwest Territory, I knew I had to be physically and mentally ready for an ordeal. To get ready, I'd been working out with weights and jogging every day— something that helped me take my mind off a lot of other troubles as well—but the real test would come in the rugged country along

16

the Divide. I'd hike and I'd climb and get used to the altitude, and when it came time to go to Canada, I wouldn't be anybody's dead weight.

That's what I told everybody, and that was the truth. At least, it was part of the truth.

The rest of the truth was that I needed the mountains, I needed to feel the wind and breathe the air and be in touch with that *other* world out there to steel myself for an ordeal that made the Mackenzie Mountains look like child's play. In a few weeks I would load up my instruments, my band and the pieces of my life, get in that big cruising bus again for the first time in a long time, and hit the road. I'd become the Hank Williams Junior Show again, and there would be audiences and articles and interviews, just like there had been for as long as I could remember. There'd be girls and groupies—snuff queens, we called 'em in country music—drugs and liquor and craziness and a whole lot of money and even more expenses. And I knew, just like always, that there'd be the people who came looking for my daddy, who wanted to hear nothing but "I'm So Lonesome I Could Cry" and "Jambalaya and a crawfish pie-a and a me-o my-o," and would be bitterly disappointed when they found only me. Just like always.

But this time, damn it, it was going to be different. This time I would be myself—I'd play Daddy's music but I'd play my music as well. This time they'd listen, and this time they'd know who I was. Damn it, this time it had to be different.

Which was enough to make me smile—well, more like grimace. Because I could feel the tension, that never-ending knot in my gut that got harder and harder, that seemed to be saying that my life had become a continuing joke. Go on the road, it said. Do your best. Give it your best shot. And when it's all over, you're still nothing but Hank Williams' kid, a novelty act, a freak, a joke. Do your darndest, then crawl back in a bottle like your daddy and do something clever, like die.

My best shot was lying in case of magnetic tape in the studios of MGM Records—the company my father's songs had built—in

Nashville. My statement. It was good. I knew it was good, and everybody who heard it knew it was good.

No, let me go a step beyond that: It was great. It was the exclamation point at the end of the old Hank Williams Junior, and the shining beginning of the new. This year, 1976, would be the beginning. I knew the album was my best shot. So why was I still all knotted up inside?

Maybe the answer was in Montana.

I use my glasses to scan the far peaks for any sign of goats while Dick rummages around in his daypack for a couple of candy bars. We'd been climbing since eight o'clock in the morning, myself, Dick and Dick's eleven-year-old son, Walt, and I'd been busting my hump just to keep up with those two. I'm in pretty good shape, but those two know the mountains like I know the frets on a guitar.

Dick's great-grandmother homesteaded this country right after the Civil War. What she found was the Big Hole, an incredible valley some eighty miles long and thirty miles wide, right in the heart of the Bitterroot Mountains. She built her cabin in the shadow of ole Ajax Mountain, struck an uneasy peace with the Nez Perce Indians, and ran her cattle in the Big Hole, keeping a wary eye out for creeping civilization. Dick's still running cattle on that land, and I think he must have inherited a lot from that old lady. He's been a champion skier, a champion snowmobile racer, and would probably be a champion at whatever he did, but he always comes back to his cabin almost within sight of that first homestead, and nearly every autumn finds him headed up the Divide, with me more likely than not tagging along.

We've been working our way along the very top of the Divide, following the brass markers hammered into the mountain to mark the continent's backbone. There's lots of good animal signs—the night before we'd spooked a couple of mule deer near the cabin—and I'm already figuring on adding another trip to Montana in a couple of months, when the hunting season opened. It's hard to believe another autumn is coming up—it's only the second week of

18

August, and in the high country the short, frantic spring has only just begun. The mountains are a riot of color, from the deep green of the woods to the exploding violet of the wildflowers, all trying to be born, grow quickly, and get ready for next spring before the snows come again.

Dick doesn't want me to know it, but he's worried about me. I can see it in the way he keeps looking back, even in the set of his mouth. He knows the tour's coming up, and I think he's one of the few people who knows what it means to me. But he won't ask: If I want to talk, he'll listen, but it's not in him to push and prod for information about my other life. It's odd how far away all that seems just now. To my left I can look off the end of the world and see the miniature village of Salmon, Idaho, nestled in the valley miles below. I have friends there, people who don't worry too much about who my daddy was and think Nashville might as well be on the moon.

Off to my right the Divide drops away thousands of feet into a high mountain valley, hidden just at the foot of Ajax's highest peak. Men came here once to look for gold; climbed ole Ajax and burrowed into its side, lowering huge buckets of ore two thousand feet down its steep sides. There are still sacks to be found in the old cabins that read "Ajax Mining Company," and the men who wander the Rockies today still make use of the old mining cabins. Through my glasses I can barely make out the red top of our jeep, parked next to one of the old cabins.

Ahead of us is old Ajax's peak, covered with a blanket of snow that has never melted. We munch our candy bars and study the trail ahead of us very carefully, 'cause no matter which way you slice it, it's a long, long way down. Dick figures we can work our way, slowly, across the snow field, over the top of Ajax, and across to some lower peaks on the other side, then work our way back down into the valley. Except for the snow fields, it's not too bad a hike, and even they shouldn't be any problem. Just watch your step.

We talk about guns and elk and how in the world did old Chief

19

Joseph of the Nez Perce ever get his people over these mountains
in the dead of winter with the U.S. Cavalry on his tail, then we sit
silent for a while. There's a trick of the mountains, that sound
doesn't always go where you want it to go. It slips away from you
and goes sliding down into the valley, and the person standing next
to you doesn't hear a word you're saying. It's eerie, sometimes.

I look up at Dick, who's watching me out of the corner of his
eye.

"I finished the album," I say, and he shakes his head happily.
"There's a song on it about Montana, and I've never sung it to people before. I mean, it's on the album, but I've never done it in a
show."

Dick and Walt are smiling expectantly.

"Would you like to hear it?"

"The heck, Hank," Dick says. He's smiling. "Get on with it!"

> I'm going to Montana to spend the winter.
> I hear the snow is deep out there and
>   the winds are cold.
> Way out there the blues will never find me.
> Oh, I'm going to Montana to rest my soul . . .

There are tiny ripples in the lake off to my left, and I imagine my
voice sliding down the mountain and slipping through the forest
like the wind. I imagine a big old elk raising his head from feeding,
shaking his immense antlers and snorting at the noise. I imagine a
sow black bear patiently explaining to her cubs that there's no need
to worry, it's just some man-thing making a racket and scaring the
game. I can feel the song inside me, and it feels like the mountains.

> I wish that special someone was going along,
> But she don't love me anymore, so I'll be gone.
> Maybe I can find someone who cares
> About the man I am, not the clothes I wear,
> 'Cause I ain't takin' nothing but my boots and jeans
> And a big ole coat along . . .

* * *

20

But, oh Lord, wouldn't her warm skin feel
   good at night?
Making love in a sleeping bag and holding
   each other tight.
We'd spend the day side-by-side, riding upon
   the Great Divide,
And look across America and feel so free inside . . .

If she'd have come with me, maybe I could have explained why I had to come. Then maybe I could explain why I did a lot of things I've done. And she could explain why she hurt me. And if she'd come with me last year, maybe we'd still have a marriage. And maybe I wouldn't have written this song. Fat chance—no chance, really.

Oh Lord that would be quite a change
   for a country boy like me.
Out there in the snow drifts, right up to my knees.
And as I warm my hands by the fire
I have to fight off a great desire
To call that girl and ask her to come out here for a while.

I'm going to Montana to spend the winter.
I hear the snow is deep out there and the winds are so cold.
'Way out where the blues will never find me,
I'm going to Montana to rest my soul.
I wish that special someone was going along.
But she don't love me anymore, so I'll be gone.
Maybe I can find someone who cares,
A sweet simple girl who'd like to share
This love I've held inside me for so long
And help me sing my Montana song . . .

The lake still ripples, and in my imagination the elk snorts and the bear laughs and the mountains are unchanging. The wind howls out of Idaho, and I just can't figure out how my life ended up such a wreck. I shake my head and grin.

"Well, whatdja think of it?" I ask. I halfway expect to hear a jeering moose.

"I think it's the best thing you've ever written, bar none," Dick replies, and I do believe he means it. "The best." Walt agrees.

And I feel good, like all the haze between here and Nashville has lifted for just a minute. We pack up our stuff and take a few minutes to take pictures of some old bleached mountain goat horns we found on the trail. Then we're on our way again.

And I can't help thinking that this moment of clarity is worth all the trouble, all the pains in the butt I had to go through to get out here. There are times when I'd like to gather up the whole music business—promoters, managers, record company honchos, flacks, the whole lousy group—and haul them up to Montana. We'd come up here to Ajax, sit around a nice fire and for once just forget all the hype, and see what we're *really* doing. I'd like to bring my wife Gwen, and my mother Audrey, and my former business manager and sit around the campfire and exorcize, once and for all, the ghost of my father, Hank Williams, Senior. I'd like to calmly explain who I am, what I do for a living, and why I don't intend to die in the back of a blue Cadillac on the way to a one-night stand in Canton, Ohio, on New Year's Day, 1953.

It seems so easy up here. We'll all smile, shake hands and exchange hugs, and everything will be fixed. I won't have been on the road since I was eight years old. I won't be billed as the reincarnation of Hank Williams, and old men won't spit on me because I don't do enough of Daddy's songs. We'll all forget about the liquor and the drugs, 'cause all that seems out of place up here anyway. I won't owe a fortune in back taxes, and I'll still have a wife I love very dearly.

Simple, see? Nothing to it. Just like taking a big old rug and shaking it until all the dust and dirt and lint goes flying up in the air and blown away by the wind. I think Daddy would appreciate the simplicity of the whole thing—he was always one to kick their asses when they weren't looking.

"Be careful, now."

That's Dick's voice, and when Dick tells you to be careful, you'd better listen *real* close. We're coming onto snow and ice over-

22

hangs, and I crawl up to the edge of one and look over. Jesus! It drops off to the edge of the world! I back away real quick. It looks like the whole thing could just drop away, and leave you hanging on the edge of nowhere with no place to go but *down*.

I'm watching my step and thinking about it, 'cause we're getting into more and more overhangs—fifty or sixty feet of snow. Only way to go is just work your way underneath them, holding on to the edge. We're just past a bad one when Dick turns around and laughs.

"I'll tell you one thing, Hank, this is the truth," Dick says. "I don't give a damn *what* John Denver says, you're the only S.O.B. in your business who's *ever* been up this high, and I'll swear to that!"

All three of us stop to laugh, and it's a good feeling.

3

I'll Never Get Out of This World Alive

There's probably been snow on top of Ajax since the day after creation, and there'll be snow there long after any of us are around to appreciate it. From the Big Hole, Ajax looks just like a postcard, a green-and-brown jagged tooth capped with white enamel, with maybe a cloud or two in a blue, blue sky to set it off. From up here on the side of Ajax, though, it just looks treacherous—a smooth white blanket of deceptively simple terrain.

All three of us pause at the top of Ajax for a powwow. There's just no way over the top without ropes and pitons and real mountaineering gear—and we simply aren't equipped. Short of turning around, which none of us wants to do, since the whole idea of this hike was to prepare for just this sort of thing in Canada, the only way to go is work ourselves down from the peak about a thousand feet, work our way around the worst of the snowdrifts, and then climb back up to the peaks and keep on hiking.

The climb up and down is not really bad at all—a little slippery, but lots of rocky handholds. What's bothering Dick is that, to work our way around the peak, we're going to have to cross a snow field about a hundred yards wide. Of all the things a casual hiker's likely to come across in these mountains, a snow field just may be the most dangerous. Even an idiot has sense enough not to harass a bear or climb a mountain in the dead of winter, but a snow field looks so *innocent*. Just a nice, flat expanse of snow, and all you've got to do is walk across it.

That's all you have to do, except that there's no way of knowing how sturdy the ground is underneath the snow, or whether the snow is melting underneath or whether it's all ice or anything.

This one looks especially scary. This whole side of Ajax is nothing but one huge rockslide, from the peak all the way down thousands of feet into the lake. There's not one square inch of solid ground, just jumbled rock from the size of your fingernail up to the size of your house. Even without snow, the footing's none too sure; one never knows if the rock you step on has been there a minute or a decade; if it's just waiting for your weight to start it rolling again.

"Just for damn sure, be careful!" Dick says, and he works his way down to the edge of the snow field. When Walt and I catch up with him, he pauses again. "I'll go first," Dick says, "Then Walt, then you, Hank."

Dick starts walking across the field. He's walking slowly, testing every step before he makes it. The ground slopes slightly toward the center of the chute, and the snow field is shaded by the peak itself. We'll work our way across, then back up. So far, so good. Dick's 165 pounds don't seem to be dislodging anything. The minutes drag on and on. He's finally across, and it seems like we've all been holding our breath forever. I smile and slap Walt on the shoulder. "Nothing to it."

"When you come across," Dick yells back across the field, "walk in my footsteps. And be damned careful not to slip, 'cause it's a long way down!"

Walt starts across, and doesn't seem to be having any trouble at all. It's amazing how clear your mind can get when there's nothing

26

but that flat expanse to concentrate on. I watch Walt and measure his every step. He steps off the field onto the rocks and waves back at me. The snow looks firm. The path is clear. I smile, wave back, and start across the field.

The snow crunches underneath my hiking boots—it feels like old snow, frozen and refrozen until it crunches like so much popcorn. I weigh about 205 pounds, and I'm packing the snow down a little deeper than Dick. After a few steps I feel a little confidence returning—no sweat, just be careful of each step. I'm almost halfway, and there's no problems at all.

I raise my right foot and lower it into Dick's footprint. The boot tread catches in the snow, and I gingerly shift my weight to that leg. I start to plan my next step when there's a tiny movement under my right foot. The rock, I think, shifted. *The rock shifted!* The movement grows, and I pull my foot away, shifting all my weight to my left leg. I step back, and feel the ground start dropping away under my left leg. Around me I see the snow shifting, the rock rearranging. I am trapped while the mountain moves. Below me, even the ripples on the lake seem frozen. I see Walt's mouth frozen in a scream. I see Dick's arms outstretched, as if he could just reach out and grab me across seventy yards of snow. The blink of an eye. A frozen breath. A heartbeat. The rocks shift. The snow slides.

And I fall.

Falling.

Like a million nightmares suddenly come true. The sick, knotted fear that explodes out of your gut and washes over your whole body, and your mind screams for you to wake up, WAKE UP!, and find the bed underneath you soaked with the sweat of falling, falling, falling.

Falling.

Frozen. Time is frozen. Your brain just refuses to let the moment go. I see everything. I see the peak. I see the lake. I see my friends. I see the rocks, and they're waiting for me. I see the snow beginning to slide underneath me, frozen. I see the Big Hole, and I see the moose and the elk and the bear. I am cold and the air is frozen. I feel the ground beginning to move again, and, oh God, I wish it would be frozen forever!

Falling.

And I am two beings. One is an animal, insane with a primeval fear, clawing at the air, gulping great draughts of air, looking frantically for escape. The other is very, very rational, a warmth that fights the insane fear. Be calm, because there's no escape. You're going to die here. You're already dead.

Falling.

I know I am dead just as surely as I've ever known anything in my life, the way that you know when you push on a door, it opens. I fall forward, and begin sliding, headfirst, down the snow chute.

"My God!" Walt screams from a million miles away. "My God! He's going to die! He's going to die!"

It's almost funny that Walt should belabor such an obvious point. Faster now; the snow burns my eyes, cuts across my face, the rocks thunder past me, and I'm calm, because it doesn't matter. I feel the rocks cutting and slashing my arms, I feel the palms of my hands shredding like papers across razor blades, feel the skin peeling away and the bones jarring, but it doesn't hurt. Through the haze of snow, I can see the lake. I am going to fall into the lake, I think.

"Turn around, Hank! Get turned around! The boulders, man! The boulders!" Dick is screaming, and he is right. I see the boulders coming up—I have been sliding a long time, the boulders were a long way away. Five hundred feet away, a thousand feet away, a city block away, and I'm almost there.

I wiggle and I struggle and I manage to turn myself around, feetfirst, heading toward the boulders. If I can just slow down. . . . I dig my heels in, and nothing happens. If I just had something to act as a brake. . . .

My gun!

The long-barreled Ruger .44, our insurance against bears, is still in the shoulder holster, still riding on my left side. If I could just get

28

the gun out, dig the barrel into the rocks. . . . But I'm a bobsled. I can barely touch the grip of the pistol with my fingers. The holster's too tight. The gun won't come out. What a joke. Maybe I can sell the holster company an endorsement, except that I'm not going to be around. All I can think of is a joke: When you're in a falling elevator, jump, just before you hit the bottom. The elevator will be wrecked, see, but you'll be okay 'cause you're up in the air—get it? My elevator has just fallen about twenty-five stories, and it's getting *real* near the bottom. Jumping makes perfect sense.

I get my feet around first and bring my knees up to my chin as far as I can. I've got on these mountain-type boots, and I can feel the rocks through the soles of my boots, and the rocks are getting bigger and bigger and there's not much time left. So I just kick out, as hard as I can.

And it works!

And I'm airborne!

Shot out of a cannon! Damn it all, it works! From a bobsled to an eagle, up, off the side of the mountain, over the boulders, and time stands very, very still. I can see the lake again, still three thousand feet below, and this time maybe I'll make it. Maybe I can make the longest swan dive in the history of the world and land in that icy lake, and maybe I won't be dead. I twist in the air, trying for more distance. I tumble, lining myself up for the dive. I see the lake slipping away from me, and as I tumble I see the snow and the rocks. I jerk and I tumble and I'm not going to make the lake. There's nothing below me but more boulders. And the eagle's going to crash.

I hit the rocks like a discarded basketball. I slide, and roll, and tumble, and everytime I seem to come down on my face, until I'm a bobsled again, only this time I'm going much faster. I slide, face forward, and the rock chips cut my chin and cheeks and the snow burns at my eyes and I can see more boulders. But I don't despair, because there's no sense despairing over the inevitable.

I am sliding, and I see it ahead of me. It's gray and ridged, sort of like a big tomahawk. I'm lined up perfect for it, as if someone started at the top of the mountain and aimed me at that gray boulder. The ridge is aimed at my nose, and I'm sliding and there's nothing I can do. In another universe Dick screams and Walt screams and I hit the boulder head-on.

What's it like . . . you remember the sound. A dull thud that goes on and on and on. Just like a hard shot in the head. I'm on my knees, and my head is down between my knees, slumped in the snow. Good God, I fell down a mountain and I'm not dead! I look at my hands, and they're still there. I always look at my hands. They're battered, but they're still there.

"I'm all right," I mumble. "I'm all right."

I am still mumbling when Dick comes down the mountain like an avenging angel. He half skis, half stumbles down old Ajax himself, and no time seems to have passed when he's by my side.

"I'm all right," I say, raising my head. "I'm all right."

Dick just stares. His eyes are wide.

"I'm all right," I say again. "I'm all right, damn it! What's wrong?"

Dick stares. "It's your nose," he finally says. "Your nose is broken."

"Then I'm going to walk off this mountain," I say. "I've got to walk off this mountain."

I stand up, and I start to take a step, but something is wrong. I sink back down to my knees.

"It's not as bad as you think, Hank," Dick is saying from someplace far away. "It's just your nose."

Walt has finally worked his way down from the peak, and I see him come running up. When he sees me, his eyes go white, and he screams and screams. It puzzles me, and I put my hands up to feel my nose. Where my nose should be there's nothing there. My teeth and parts of my jaw fall out in my hand. I raise my hand to my forehead, and where my forehead should be, there's something soft and squishy. That's my brain, I think.

I have no face.

"What is it?" I say to Dick. "What is it?"

My cheek is gone. My eye is hanging down. My head is shattered, and the warm stuff I feel is my blood. "Oh, God," I think. "Oh, dear God. After all this, the mountain's going to win anyway."

"It's not that bad, Hank, but you can't walk off the mountain," Dick is saying. I look close with my one good eye, and there's a tear on Dick's cheek, which is sort of funny because everybody knows cowboys don't cry. "It's just your nose."

Dick lays me down in the snow and takes my hands away from my face. He has decisions to make. He takes his hand—"his dirty ole hand," he says later—and pushes my exposed brain back into my head. It makes a terrible sound, a nightmare sound that nobody can hear but me. I'll always hear that sound. Then he takes the shredded pieces of my face and pushes them back where they're supposed to be, and he whips off his shirt and ties it around my head. Then he steps back and looks at me.

From someplace far away I can see a lot of things in my friend's eyes. I can see a deathwatch, and I could see that he had a tough decision to make. Go, or stay. He knows that I'm finished. I see that with perfect clarity, just as plainly as I could see the lake while I was tumbling in the air.

In a flash, the decision is made.

"Walt, you're going to have to stay here with Hank while I go for help," Dick says.

"No." Walt is horrified. "I can't do it."

"You have to."

"He's going to die, and I'm not going to stay here with him!"

"Walt, if he's got a chance in the world, I'm going to have to go," Dick says. "It's got to be me."

Walt finally agrees, and I hear it all. I don't really have an opinion one way or the other. It was a question, Dick says later, of whether to stay with your best friend while he was dying or take the long shot. He doesn't know why he took the long shot, only that a feeling came over him that he had to *take* it.

I lie in the snow while Dick and Walt confer. Walt is shaken, but he's an awful tough eleven-year-old.

"Whatever you do, don't let him go to sleep," Dick says. "You've got to keep him talking. If he goes to sleep, he's dead for sure. Just keep him talking."

4

Standing in the Shadows

Damned odd, I think, to be lying on this mountain waiting to die and to be surrounded by a couple of giants. Two giants, and if I think hard, I can put my finger on who they are. Dick. Walt. They are bigger than I am, not in size, but in dimension. They are *more* than I am; they're competing with the mountains. They loom over me with worried faces; they talk to each other about me. Dick is going to stride down the mountain—giants don't have to worry about falling, I don't think—and he's going to come back with help. Not that it matters all that much.

The other giant, Walt, is going to stay and talk to me, and it would be terribly rude of me to not make some effort to pay attention, although what I really want to do is sleep. Maybe Walt has something important to say—one can never tell.

"Hank," Dick the giant is saying. "Hank."

He kneels beside me, and when he kneels, he shrinks to almost human size. I try to tell him, but it's not really important.

"Hank, I'm going down the mountain to get help," Dick says. "I've got to go for help. Now, Walt's going to stay here with you,

33

and he's going to talk to you to keep you company, and everything's going to be just fine. Understand?"

Of course I understand. What's to understand? I am irritated, but not much.

"Okay, now just don't worry. I'll be back as soon as I can."

I am not worried. I am lying in the snow, and Dick thinks I should be lying somewhere else. That's okay with me, so I try to stand up and walk somewhere else, but my legs aren't exactly working. Dick and Walt carry me to some higher ground, which is all rocks and no snow—not much of an improvement, if you ask me.

Dick lays me facedown, and my blood drips onto the rocks and trickles down into the mountain. I think that someday someone might find those rocks and wonder how they came to be that color. It is nice, though, because with my one eye that still works, I can look across the high valley. I can see the peaks, and I can see the lake. On the whole, it's a good view. And I'm going to sleep.

Only Walt is talking.

What he's talking about is fish, and I can't think of anything I'm less interested in at this moment than fish. Brook trout.

"I guess I musta caught fifty, maybe seventy-five of these l'il ole brook trout, you know, about as big as your hand. But they're real good eatin', you know. Mom fries them up in the morning for breakfast and we must eat up twenty or thirty of them every time we sit down for breakfast, and I guess the secret of it is these little bitty black flies that them trout just go nuts over, you know? You know, Hank? You do a lot of trout fishing, Hank?"

Uh-huh, I say, because it would be really impolite not to say anything.

"I got this great move with the rod, and that ole black fly just jumps around, and those trout can't let it go. Can't resist it, no sir. You ever been in one of those fishing holes where you just can't miss, Hank? Where those trouts just beg you to catch them? Hank?"

Uh-huh. I don't think Walt has seen just how banged up I am—

34

that's the only way to explain this conversation. He doesn't know that I'm going to die, and he doesn't know that he's going to end up on this godforsaken mountain with a corpse. I feel sorry for him.

His voice is like the wind, blowing up from Idaho. I hear them come howling over the mountain, to break on a little rock dam that Walt has constructed around my head. The wind and Walt—both of them kind of fade away; they move to a different place. Not really. It's easy to forget . . .

"I'll never forget, we had this ole coon dog, and it was the darndest thing, this ole dog. He'd run them coons right until . . ."

We're on the dark side of the mountain, the peak of old Ajax shielding us from what's left of the late-afternoon sun. It's okay, though, because up here the sun doesn't have any strength anyway. I can see the sun, though, over there across the lake. I can see the ripples on the lake, and from 'way across the lake comes this feeling. It's almost time, now. I try to say something real profound, like "Hank, you're dying. This is it," but I can't. I can't really talk at all.

It's odd, you know, but I've wanted to die a lot of times. I tried to kill myself once, and I even screwed that up. I've wanted to die a lot, but I never wanted to die on this godforsaken mountain. I never wanted to die on some old mountain. It's just not *musical* enough, damn it. I mean, I'm not opposed to the idea of *dying*: I've got nothing to live for, I guess, so what difference does that make? But dying ought to be classy, like in some motel room on the road, or even on stage—now that would really be doing it up right. Just get up there on that stage, under all those lights, pick up that old guitar and die, deader than a brick. My daddy had style, and I always figured I'd go something like that, in the back seat of a Cadillac on the way to another show in Nowhere, Ohio.

But this is real, I think. The real thing is on this mountainside, and I can feel it coming. I wonder if Walt can feel it creeping up through these rocks. I sort of hope he can't.

"The basketball team was okay, but I'm really looking forward to football, see. I'm not big enough to be a fullback or something like that, but I can run real good and catch passes and I think I'd make a great tight end or something, don't you, Hank? Whatdaya think, Hank, an end or what?''

I am alone on this mountain, and I have been alone all my life. I hear and see and feel, but I think my mind has disconnected me from all that, because there are more important things to be decided this afternoon.

There are pictures in my mind, a hand turning the pages of a photo album. I think it's interesting that your life doesn't exactly flash before you; it's more like machine-gun thoughts, sort of a reviewing process. Sort of going through your baggage for a long trip, and picking out what you'd like to take with you. It's just me and you, God, I think—maybe just a little sarcastically, maybe not—and I've still got some thinking to do.

I think of my son, Shelton, who was going to grow up without a daddy anyway.

I think of my wife, Gwen, who's told me she doesn't love me anymore, and I can't get that through my thick head.

I think of my mother, who loves me too much, and I forgive her what she did, and I think I understand a little, too. I wish she would forgive me for things I did.

I think of my daddy, and I think I owe him some kind of explanation, which is important, because I'm going to be seeing him soon.

I try to think of some way to start out that doesn't seem too trite. I have all the time in the world, and my thoughts drift away. I see my friends, my few friends who love me whether I'm Hank Williams Junior or not. There's Dick who's climbing down the mountain, and Bill Dyer who's my hunting buddy in Tennessee, and J. R. Smith, good ole Robert, who's my new manager and who told me maybe I wasn't fated to go to Montana and now won't have much to manage.

My friend Merle Kilgore is crazy, and he's never going to forgive me for this. It's enough to make him quit drinking. He remembers my daddy, and I think things would have been different if Daddy had lived.

An Autobiography

If he'd lived, then maybe I wouldn't have to have tried so hard to become him; sing his songs and practice his patter. Mother used to coach me, when I was just a little kid. She'd coach me in things Daddy said and then I'd go out on stage and the audience would go crazy. They'd say I sounded just like ole Hank, and I guess I did.

That's what it's like, Daddy, and I guess that's what I've got to say. I mean, I tried, standing there in front of the mirror and singing along with your records, trying to get it down just like you did, every catch, every wail. I wanted to be just like you, because it was important that I was just like you. People wanted me to be just like you. Mother wanted me to be just like you. I wanted it so bad.

Did I ever tell you that one time I made it with this girl singer on the bus driving over to meet my wife? Did you ever do stuff like that? On the way to meet Mother?

But there's my own music, and it's in there trying to get out. There's my album back in that can in Nashville. And I'm getting better—what a joke, at least, I was getting better—but the demons, Daddy, I can't seem to shake the demons. They gnaw at me and claw at me and tell me that it all turns to dust, that I'm nothing but the son of a bum, the weak son of a bum who was better than I'll ever be. People have spit on me because I wasn't you, Daddy. Have hated me, and snarled at me, and wanted to slap my face and I don't understand. I never understood.

But it's comfortable here, and it's warm, and the sun is starting to set. Just like lying on a soft couch and watching some favorite television show and just drifting off to sleep. And if there's nothing on television, why, I can just step back and watch that man lying on those rocks, and watch that little boy sitting next to him talking his head off. That's pretty entertaining, really, and I watch them for a while, and I watch the sun going down. It's a weak sun, and the wind is howling out of Idaho.

Oh Lord, I think, I don't pray very much I know, but the least You could have done is to arrange something better than this old mountain.

Maybe there's a scale in each of us that balances between life and death. And maybe the center of that balance is God. And maybe I'm never going to be a religious man, maybe there are too many bird hunts and trout streams and any God worth His salt would have to understand that—and maybe, God, I just don't want to die on this mountain. Maybe, God, I just don't want to die at all. I just don't know.

Dr. Metz.

The name pops into my mind unbidden. Dr. Metz, my friend, my counselor. He told me to start being a mean son-of-a-bitch. That's what he told me to do. No more ole Hank'll take care of this; ole Hank'll take care of that. You've got to be a mean son-of-a-bitch.

Whadda You think about that, God?

What do You think about living?

Quiet now, and my thoughts touch the blurred photographs for the last time. Quiet now, and I am sleepy and I am bored with watching the man on the mountain and the boy talking to him. It's time to sleep.

But . . .

But still . . .

And there is a part of me that glows, that scares away the darkness where it touches. And I look at the glowing and I pray, I really pray.

I'm not worthy, Lord, but I want to live. The glow strengthens and flares, and it's suddenly so clear. I know who I am.

I know who I am.

I know *what* I am.

And I can feel the despair roll away from me like quilts on a cold morning. I can feel the self-loathing peel away from me.

Life.

But there's no bolt from the blue, raising me up and making me whole, no splitting of the clouds or angel chorus to carry me away.

Just the mountain.

I'm alone on this mountain.

And I'm dying.

The despair comes like a savage animal—to find your soul and

38

lose your life in the same afternoon! I look across the lake, and sleep is both seductive and insistent. Come, it says, let go. Rest.

And I pray.

I look across the lake, and my eye focuses on my hand. I look at it for a while, then I notice my two rings. Two diamond initial rings. H. W. Hank Williams. The most famous name in country music. My daddy's rings. There's nobody here but me and God and two diamond rings.

I lift my hand experimentally, and I'm surprised to see that my hand actually moves. It raises, maybe an inch, maybe two. I hold it there for a second, then I weaken and let it drop.

Thud!

A sound. A beat. A heartbeat. So quiet that you could barely hear it, but so loud it shook my entire being.

Again I raise my hand, and my eye watches the two diamond rings. Again, I let it drop.

Thud!

The sleep shudders and backs away a step! The sound rings and reverberates through my soul, the sound of iron striking iron, my chorus of angels.

Thud!

Thud!

Thud!

And I know. I know that as long as I can hear the beat, I'm in this world.

Thud!

Thud!

It *is* a heartbeat! It is my living heartbeat, and it echoes through the rock, across the mountain until the very clouds seem to ring with its magnificence.

I live.

"So we were hunting this muley deer, and we'd been tracking the bunch of them for a long time when we finally jumped them and—please don't die, Hank. Don't die. I know you're going to be all right . . ."

I hear Walt, and he's still talking. There are tears rolling down his face, and it's almost dark on the mountain. I feel the cold creeping in, around the edges of my warm cocoon. I know the pain can't be far behind, and I know it's going to be bad. Death thwarted will want his revenge.

"Walt!" There's a shout from down in the valley, and I think it's Dick! He's back! Has it really been hours? Could it have been? "Walt! Is Hank alive?"

Inside, I almost laugh.

"Dad! Dad!" Walt yells, and the mountains echo. "He's still talking! He's alive!"

When Dick makes it back to the ledge, the pain is just beginning, and he can't understand why I'm beating on the ground like some kind of madman.

5

I Saw the Light

There are parts of the story I can't tell, parts I didn't even know until days, months, even years later. I knew Dick Willey had come back. What I didn't know were the details of his own ordeal, a frenetic race down the face of Ajax to find help, sick with the knowledge that his own son might be sitting on the mountain with a corpse.

As Dick told me later:

"It took me about twenty minutes to get to the car that's down the face of a steep mountain, alongside the lake to an old mining cabin, and that's no small hike. By then you're just running scared. All these things are just running through your mind. You're thinking, God, why did we ever go up on the mountain? Why did he have to fall? How am I going to tell his mother that I let her son die? And you're running over logs and rocks—I must have fallen many times trying to leap over fallen logs."

He finally made it to the car, a Toyota Land Cruiser station wagon with four-wheel drive. The drive down Ajax is along an old fire trail. On a good day the trail is almost as wide as a jeep. Almost.

41

And it's steep enough to cause a mountain goat to gulp. On those good days you can watch the rocks overturned by your tires roll off the side of the mountain, take a couple of bounces, and drop away into oblivion. More than one jeep has joined those rocks.

"I jumped in that son-of-a-gun and away I went. It's a fifteen-mile-an-hour road if you know it real well. There were times I was going eighty. Once you reach the forest at the base of the mountain, it's a good twelve miles until there's even any *sign* of civilization. And once you get to the first signs, it's another ten miles until you get back to my cabin. I figured the only thing I could do was get back to the cabin, call the Forest Service, call *somebody*. Anyway, I'm going down the road just as fast as I can go, go hauling into this turn, and wreck."

Two years later Dick told me that he'd wrecked the car trying to get help. He hadn't wanted to bother me with it before.

"I thought, 'My God, what else can go wrong?' What happened was I came around this turn and of course it's a gravel road, and I got to sliding. I smashed into the side of a bridge, which threw me back across the road into a creekbed, about ten feet deep. I didn't know what else to do, so I got the sucker in four-wheel-drive—and this bank must be almost straight up. I backed off and hit the bank. And hit it again. And I'll be darned if that rascal didn't come out of there. And I just headed on along what we call the foothills road—I still had about ten miles to go when as luck would have it, I ran into a Forest Service vehicle."

Luck.

I didn't know much about luck right then. Later, I'd have a lot of time to think about my luck, if you want to call it that. Forest Service vehicles are few and far between. You could drive for months along those fire roads and never see another vehicle, much less a Forest Service one. Luck, eh?

"So he radioed back to Forest Service headquarters that there had been an accident on Ajax and that it was going to take a helicopter to get to the victim. So I stayed there until he did confirm that there would be a helicopter. I was there for about forty-five minutes. Then I took off. I headed back up the mountain. From the time I left Hank until the time I got back, I guess it took me a little over two hours.''

Two hours. Could that have been all?

"So I left the jeep and started back up, and I just knew by then he'd had it. So I get to the far end of the lake, and I could see Walt, way up there, just a speck. So I hollered up to Walt, about a half a mile up, just as loud as I could. I yelled, 'Is Hank okay?' And, by golly, he yelled back, 'Yea!' I hollered again, 'Is Hank still alive?', and Walt yelled 'Yes!' I just couldn't believe it! So anyway, I rushed up the mountain and he's still conscious and seems to be fairly comfortable. So I reassured him again that the helicopter was coming, that he only had a broken nose, and that everything was fine.''

There is a point, I think, where your life is finally constricted to a tiny white-hot flame that doesn't much care for the outside world. It observes, but it does so without comment. So it is on the mountain—things go on around me, and I watch and record. There is a helicopter coming, and Dick has come back, and I know that is good. Dick is talking to Walt, and they're both watching me pretty closely, pausing their conversation to reassure me. I accept their reassurances and record them somewhere inside.

Something else is happening inside—pain. I feel sharp stabbings and aches from my body, from my face. I accept the pain, and I know it's going to get worse, much worse. There is, I think, a certain irony here, perhaps a lesson to be learned. The more alive I am, the more I hurt. The more I expand from that single point of consciousness, the more tiny activity of my arms and legs, the more twitches, the more pain I feel.

It's like waking up from a particularly pleasant dream or crawling out from under a warm quilt into a cold room. I've been given life, and now I'm going to have to pay the price.

It all comes down to waiting, and waiting's still not that hard. You concentrate on your body. You take a mental inventory—

fingers all work, toes all work, arms twitch—and work toward aligning yourself with the real world. It is cold, and I feel the cold for the first time. I watch Dick and Walt and a couple of campers who seemed to have joined the party work on the rock wall Walt started building around me. Pretty soon the wall is three feet high, and I don't feel the cold nearly as bad. Time passes.

I can hear the helicopter from a long way off. The helicopter! I feel excitement for the first time. I am tired of this mountain. I have fought my battle here, and I am impatient to get on with the other battles that are waiting. And the pain, the pain is a constant gnawing now and I am impatient and sulky. I want off this mountain!

The helicopter circles once, and everybody is yelling and waving. The helicopter doesn't land, but starts instead to go away. The yelling takes on a desperate sound, and the helicopter, as if it heard and relented, turns back, circles again, and starts looking for a place to alight. They find the only flat space in the rocks, about 200 feet away, and the helicopter sets down. There is a medic, and his name is Swede Thorenson, he says, and he asks me, "How ya doin', pal?" Just fine, I say. Just fine. Actually, I snap, because it's a stupid question and it's that much longer before I get off the mountain. I don't think he noticed that I snapped. I don't think I can talk very well. Maybe I can't talk at all. Swede asks me other questions, and I don't think I answer him.

He changes the dressings on my head. It hurts this time. There's a prick in my arm, and the pain goes away a little. There's another prick in another place and something starts trickling into my body. This is good, I think, because I can see the drying puddles of my blood, and there are lots of puddles. I don't think I can afford all those puddles.

All that remains between me and getting off this mountain is 200 feet of rock, and they strap me in the stretcher and start the trip.

It's a nightmare!

The rocks are huge and unforgiving, and I'm strapped into the

44

stretcher. My feet are raised. My head is lowered. And I'm in agony! Up, down, up down up down. I can't understand why it's taking so long. Twenty minutes it takes. Ten times longer than it took me to fall. We are at the helicopter, and they are strapping me to the *outside*. I don't want to be on the outside. I want to be on the inside, where it's warm, where there's no wind and no pain. I complain, but no one understands. Swede climbs into the helicopter with the pilot. I hear the motor rev, faster and faster, and the helicopter gives a little lurch. It rises an inch, hovers for a second, and is then airborne for real.

I am off the mountain, alive.

It's cold and I'm trying to figure out a way to get my right knee out of these damn straps! I feel like one giant bruise, from my knees to my chest to my back, and I know that if I can just get my knee out of the strap and bring it up, I can stop this pain. I struggle and I scream and I hurt—Lord, I hurt! My leg hurts. My thigh hurts. All I can concentrate on is breaking the straps—I am not worried about gravity. I know that if I break the straps, I'll somehow avoid falling off the helicopter. I am still struggling and screaming when the helicopter lands at a nearby ranch with an airstrip, and there's a small plane waiting to ferry me to the hospital at Missoula.

Which is much better. Swede is talking to me now, telling me how I'll be all right. I'm still trying to get the straps off my legs—I can't seem to get across how badly my legs hurt, how much I want to curl up. Swede's holding up those bottles that are dripping into me. It seems to take a long time to get to Missoula, over a hundred miles away, but when we get there another helicopter is waiting, this time for the short trip to Community Hospital. Even through the pain I marvel about how organized these guys are. I congratulate myself for having the good sense to fall off a mountain with all these guys around.

I see the big red cross below, the hospital landing pad, and we set down again. All those people in white come swarming out of the hospital, and I'm being unstrapped and loaded into a different stretcher.

"You got it, buddy," one of the medics says. "You're going to be okay."

"You want us to call someone? And I think about it. My mother is sick, maybe dying, and if she isn't dying, this should just about do it. My wife is just more pain. My friends are after my money. Dick cares, and he already knows. Maybe I shouldn't bother anyone else with my problems. Maybe I've spent my whole life bothering other people with my problems. Maybe that's what I learned up on that mountain.

"You want us to call someone, buddy?"

"No!" I almost shout, and the attendant jumps back startled. No!

Then I'm on my way to the operating room, with them cutting away on my clothes all the while. Just like that, my boots and jeans are cut off; my bloody jacket and the shoulder holster with the gun that wouldn't come out, snipped through like so much tissue paper. I must look like some kinda outlaw, I think, with my head all bloody and that gun and holster with all the bullets in it. They cut off my belts and my underwear. Then they cut off my cross I was wearing around my neck: the cross that had been with me through charging elephants and stalling planes. I didn't know why I was wearing it when I went on the mountain, but I beg them not to cut it off. I tell them I know what it means now, and to please leave it on.

Snip.

They wash me and prep me and I watch, pretty interested. I am clean and warm and not in too much pain at all when the nurse comes with another needle. Sodium pentothal, she says. You're going to go to sleep, she says, and sticks the needle in.

It is seven thirty in the evening, August 8, 1975, almost eight hours since I started across a snowfield on the side of old Ajax. I am Hank Williams Junior, the son of a legend, and I am alive. Thank God.

46

That said, I go to sleep, finally.

There are parts of the story I can't tell, how three surgeons who just happened to be in the hospital on a Saturday—instead of at their house on the lake, ninety miles away—spent seven and one-half hours putting me back together again. Dr. Don Murray, Dr. Tom Holshaw, Dr. Richard Dewey working on the remains of my face, cleaning out the wounds, suturing, saving what they could. They thanked the cold on the mountains for keeping down the infection. They added the pluses of my youth and good condition. They added their skill, and they decided that I had a chance. When they came out of the operating room, Dick told me later, they looked like they'd been through the mill. They looked worse than I did.

I wake up in the Intensive Care Unit late the next day, and the first thing I notice is the nurse, which, I think, is probably a good sign. There is something in my throat, a breathing tube, I think. There are needles in my arms, and my jaws are wired together. I move my tongue around, and the inside of my mouth is all a maze of wires and plastic stuff and braces. My head is swollen up like a watermelon, and I explore the wreckage of my mouth with my tongue. The nurse leans close, and her nameplate says "Fitzgerald."

"You've had a bad mountain fall, Mr. Williams," she says. "You're in Community Hospital in Missoula, Montana, and we're going to take care of you. Do you understand?"

I think they're worried about whether there's anything left in my head except wire and plastic.

"Um-huh," I say, and that's as much as I can say. I'm suddenly very, very tired, and as I go to sleep, I hear the machinery of the Unit. It sounds reassuring.

In the morning come the doctors. They have lots to tell me, but what I really want is ice. My mouth is filled with the gritty, coppery

47

taste of blood, and I want to gargle and spit it out. Except that my jaws are wired shut, and there's this little hole where they can squirt medicine and maybe a little ice through. They have this stuff I have to take, stuff to fight an infection of the brain that the doctors *have* to talk to me about, and the only way to take it is orally, through a large syringe. So they squirt it through the hole, and it tastes *awful, terrible, vile*! And I get lots of it, because that's what the doctors are worried about.

Well, it's one of the things the doctors are worried about. I'm lucky with doctors—Dick Dewey, my neurosurgeon, spent two tours in Vietnam, and he'd seen a lot of bullet holes and bone fragments. Dr. Holshaw, the eye, ear, nose, and throat man, is going to have a field day, finding me a new eye, ear, nose, and throat. And then, of course, Don Murray, the plastic surgeon, is probably facing a challenge of a lifetime, and he is certainly up to it.

Imagine, they tell me, a chart of the human skull with all the bones in the face displayed. Every single one of those bones was broken—every single one. The probable reason you're not dead, they say, is that the front of your face—the jaws, the gums, the teeth, the nose, even the forehead—cushioned the brain from the blow. Unfortunately, the cushions were destroyed. Also unfortunately, the human brain isn't designed to be exposed to the elements, much less shoved around on a godforsaken mountaintop. When the brain is exposed, an infection invariably—almost invariably—results, with fatal results.

In other words, they say, you're off the mountain, but you're not out of the woods. Not by a long shot.

I can see the snow on the mountaintops out the window. I look out and watch the clouds roll by. Dr. Dewey just shakes his head. "I don't see how you survived," he says. "But you did. You did."

So we settle into routine, quickly. I've lost a lot of my sight, all my sense of smell and taste, some of my hearing. There are tubes down my throat, needles in my arm, monitors hooked all over. I have my rings, and when I need a shot for the pain, I tap on the side

48

of the bed, against the metal rail. Nurses and doctors ask me questions, and I write answers on a little pad. Routine.

Soon the word gets out, south to Nashville. I am near death, the reports say. But I don't think I'm near death; I've been near death, and I've got a pretty good idea of what it's like. My wife comes to my bedside, and she looks tired. Gwen, my wife, comes, and she says she still loves me, and it's all been a horrible mistake. Sure, I write. Sure. I want to believe her, but I've heard that song before.

Dick and Betty and Walt are here, as is Bill Dyer and his wife Betty, and J.R. Smith, my manager and friend. I believe in them, and I hope they'll head off the shitstorm that's headed for Missoula, Montana. It's going to be a circus, I think, a real three-ring circus.

If I make it eight days, the doctors tell them, I'll live.

Eight days.

One week and a day.

Oh God, everyone wails. And they all settle down to wait a week and a day.

6

Star-Maker Machinery

Let me tell you a little about country music, something I guess I know a bit about—not necessarily through any choice of my own. It's easy to think of country music as some kind of monolith: Country Music; the Kingdom of Nashville; the Grand Ole Opry; all that stuff. And that's part of it to be sure. But there's a whole other side of country music that most of you never get to see, and that's the business side.

Country music isn't like it was in the old days—if there was ever any such thing as the old days, which I've come to doubt. The reason it's different is simple: money. We're not talking about some quaint Smoky Mountain folk music or some weird cowboy songs that only a handful of people listen to. We're talking about a multimillion-dollar industry with tendrils that stretch across the country. One monster hit can mean, literally, millions of dollars. In my daddy's time, *The Wall Street Journal* felt it necessary to comment on the fact that a "hillbilly singer" could make as much as $100,000 a year. At the time, that was big news. Now, it wouldn't even rate a comment in somebody's gossip column—a new touring bus can cost twice that amount, and some country acts are touring with two buses and two semi-trucks to carry the sound equipment. What we're talking about here is *big* money.

The real problem is that the artist—me, for instance—has to straddle the fence between the smiling good ole boy in coveralls who learned to strum the guitar on the lower forty, and the professional businessman in a three-piece suit and a Yale education, who can figure cash-flow for the next five years and knows more about small print than a miniature Bible salesman.

The thing that has traditionally made country music different from, say, pop, is that the country singer is (or has always been) a *part* of his audience, just a good ole boy or girl who happened to make it good and who never forgot how he or she came to be a star. Ernest Tubb, who's had his share at the top of the charts, is fond of saying that he doesn't do anything that the next ole boy couldn't do just as well. And maybe in some kind of spiritual sense that's true. But remember this: No one gives up a home and a family and any vague sense of security to spend 300 nights a year, nine out of every ten days, year-in, year-out, in the back of some Silver Eagle bus on the way to some honky-tonk in the middle of nowhere unless that person *believes*, totally believes with every ounce of his soul and his heart and his mind, that he has something special to offer.

Merle Kilgore, who has been on the road with me for twelve *looooong* years, has his own theory about it:

"Artists love popularity," Merle says in that gravel-throated voice that sounds sort of like cold molasses being poured over hot rocks. "Being in the top ten, all that bullshit—everybody loves you. Forget all the causes and effects. Forget all the 'I'm recording this song for such-and-such reason.' Bullshit. When you're sitting up there on the top ten, baby, and your picture's in every magazine there is, and you're in demand and everybody loves you—you love it! It feeds your ego and you live on that ego. If I didn't have it, I'd a-quit a *long* time ago. Shit, I'd'a blown a million dollars, and I'd a-killed myself, if I'd'a been a human."

Merle's stone cold right, too.

An Autobiography

We send out a million press releases a year to explain to our fans that we're the same as they are; with the same roots, dreams, goals, and aspirations. You believe us, and, in turn, you demand that familiarity from us. You insist that we be good ole boys and girls. And for a long time that worked just fine. When the Grand Ole Opry first started, the performers used to come to WSM's radio studios wearing three-piece suits. Before they went on the air, they changed into frayed coveralls and checked gingham shirts.

We tell our story in the press, and we're careful to emphasize that we're just one of the guys. (Bill Anderson, when he came to Nashville with a degree in journalism, felt obliged to hide that fact. It was a definite hindrance.) Sometimes, we ourselves come to believe the wall of myth that we manage to erect around ourselves. Sometimes it makes perfectly good sense to think you're the reincarnation of your father; that you're ordained for stardom because of some genetic quirk. But maybe I'm getting ahead of my story a little bit.

We surround ourselves with hype, but we know, for the most part, just exactly what it is. Which makes it that much harder on us in the long run. Don't get me wrong—I'm not singing the "Got Dem Old Cosmic Entertainer Blues." Not too much, anyway. But I think it's important to realize that there is a difference between the guy down the street who sings for his girlfriend and the professional entertainer who sings for thousands of people almost every night of the year. That difference is ego.

So we try to deal with our egos and the record company executives at the same time. We have strategy meetings and we plot our careers for the next five years. We discuss product—that's the music—packaging, and marketing strategies. We discuss giant paper cutouts, press parties, and trade magazine charts. We worry about who's getting a cut of the money from publishing our original songs. We worry about our managers, our publicists, and our fans. Sometimes we worry about the Internal Revenue Service, and we decide to become professional wilderness guides or some other obscure occupation. But we never do.

All the time we're making our plans and worrying ourselves sick

53

about every tiny aspect of our careers, the very nature of the country music business is changing underneath us. I compare it to trying to play golf on a giant turntable—just about the time you think you've got it all figured out, somebody speeds up or slows down the turntable and *WHAMMO*, you're back to Square One. Most recently, country music has been like a turntable that's iced over—nothing seems to hold true for longer than a couple of months, just like the pop music business.

In a lot of ways, I feel vindicated. I mean, it seems like Nashville is finally coming around to the kind of music I've been doing for years. Only now they call it "pop crossover," which means, simply, that the song has a chance to "cross over" to another chart, from the country chart to the pop charts. That's the difference between selling 100,000 records on a good day and selling 1,000,000 records on a bad one. And that difference'll keep you in shotgun shells for a long time, cousin. A song like "Rainy Night in Georgia," which I recorded several years ago, would be a perfect crossover song—not *too* traditionally country, but with a very broad appeal. That's the good part.

The bad part is that Nashville, typical to its nature, can't do *anything* in moderation. The powers-that-be (And, oh Lord, have I fought it!) can't seem to see that there's more to country music than what's hot this afternoon. If pop crossover sells, then, by God, everybody ought to be cutting pop crossover! Forget the individual's talent and personal style. Haul their asses into the studio and let's see if we can cut tomorrow's pop hit. It's a factory mentality, and it's a mentality that's hurt Nashville and the acceptance of country music time and time again. I'll be damned if I'll be a part of it. Sometimes I think I'll probably be damned.

I should tell the story of a good friend of mine who's been something of an inspiration to me. I tell you this because Waylon Jennings faced off with the system and the system lost, and sometimes when I'm especially depressed, I can't help but think that Waylon did it, and I can do it too. It's a story that has its roots in Nashville's total bullheadedness, and it begins in a roundabout way, with Chet Atkins.

54

An Autobiography

Chet came to Nashville in the early 1950s as a sessions player—a man who plays an instrument in a recording session. The fact that he was already one of the world's great guitarists didn't hurt one bit, and in no time he was a power in Music City. He eventually ended up as head of RCA Records, one of the most powerful labels in Nashville, and he was in a unique position to impose his personal viewpoint on a whole generation of country musicians.

His own viewpoint was no less unique—he wasn't that interested in traditional country music, the steel guitars and what had come to be called the high lonesome sound of my father's music. Chet was more interested in jazz, and in orchestral background, in experimenting. Which would not be such a big deal, except that, as I said earlier, the industry is always changing. Country music had just been nearly totally wiped out by the birth of rock and roll (in the very womb of country music, which I always thought was *very* interesting), and the powers-that-be of that particular time, the late 1950s and early 1960s, saw country's salvation in the sprawling suburbs.

Chet Atkins' softer country music seemed just the ticket for those suburbs. And it worked like crazy. They called it the Nashville Sound, and I'd be a liar if I told you I didn't benefit from it. But just like today's pop crossover mania, Nashville refused to accept the idea that *anything* but the Nashville Sound had a right to be recorded. Waylon didn't care much for the Nashville Sound: He'd been a member of Buddy Holly's Crickets and had come out of rocking West Texas musical tradition. What he wanted to play was his own music. Nashville was monumentally uninterested.

The sixties ground into the seventies, rock rose and fell a couple of times, and country music held to the cherished myth of the Nashville Sound. Waylon held on to his music. To make a long story short, Waylon won. He read the audience better than the music mogols in Nashville. He knew in his gut that not everybody wanted to hear the same set of violins behind songs that seemed to sound exactly the same. And now every one of his songs is a number one song. The music's the same as it always was—no frills, no violins, no Nashville Sound, no concessions.

55

I once gave Waylon a pair of my daddy's boots, because I knew what the story of my daddy's life meant to Waylon. It was right after Waylon wrote a song called "Are You Sure Hank Done It This Way?", which asked a question I'd faced every day of my life. I think that song meant as much to me as it did to Waylon. So I gave Waylon a pair of my daddy's boots, 'cause I knew they'd mean something to him. The next time I saw him, he was grinning like a sheepish little boy.

"You tried 'em on, didn't you?" I asked. Waylon just grinned like he was looking for a rock to kick. "I knew you would, you S.O.B. you."

"Yea," Waylon said. "And they fit, too."

So Waylon beat 'em, and I can't tell you what that meant to me. Because if Waylon could beat 'em, I could beat 'em. There is safety in numbers, you know. At least, there's a little reassurance. Perhaps the biggest danger that any performer faces is the creeping fear that he's totally alone. That there's nobody else out there who knows how you feel or what you want or what it's like. When you spend your life in the back of a bus, that's an easy thing to think. It's easy to look at that bunk, which looks suspiciously like a coffin, and feel the road rolling by underneath you and wonder what in the hell you're doing.

Seems like there's all the time in the world to think, and the only things you can think of are bad. Especially if your last name is Williams, and when your father thought about all those things, he ended up dead in the back seat of a Cadillac. The wheels hum, the air conditioner makes a little sound, the band laughs and tells jokes or maybe argues—after twenty or thirty hours of that, you could come to believe anything. Especially that you're all alone, and everything outside isn't really real.

That's country music, folks, and that's what killed my father and almost killed me. I thought you ought to know.

7

Daddy

There are pictures in my mind—not quite memories—of Daddy. More like snapshots without any captions.

Once on an airplane, his long, lanky frame sprawled out on the floor. He wasn't wearing a hat, and he was balding.

Once at an early morning radio show in Nashville, or maybe backstage at the Opry. Backstage somewhere, anyhow. And I knocked over a speaker baffle, crawling around. And I caught pure hell for it. I remember the place was packed, and Daddy was all decked out, fit to kill—big white hat and big five-inch tie, looking good. The audience just went crazy.

Finally, at our house on Franklin Road in Nashville. He's lying on the couch with his hat off, and I noticed his thin hair again. One wisp of black and all thin. I was sitting on the floor, beating on the furniture with a hammer. When I got older, people asked me what happened to Daddy's furniture to cause all those marks.

Those are the only three pictures I have in my mind of my father. Sometimes other images float through—nights on the road; Mother, Daddy and me, backstage and happy—but I can't decide whether they're real pictures or images created by my mind to tell me about the father I never knew.

I do know this: Daddy's and my life are diametrically opposed. His life was the stuff of which country songs are made. His was up from poverty; mine is down from wealth.

He was born September 17, 1923, just outside of the little town of Georgiana, Alabama, which is some sixty miles south of Montgomery. By all rights, that's where he should have stayed.

From the beginning, luck wasn't with him. His father, a sometimes locomotive engineer, sometimes berry picker, had been shell-shocked during World War One, and by the time Daddy was seven, his father had checked into the Veterans Hospital and out of Daddy's life for good. The chore of raising the boy fell to Lilly Williams, his mother. She played gospel piano at her local church, and Hank used to sit on the big bench with her while she played.

But times were hard, and Lilly responded in what must be a novel way for a southern woman—she decided to move to Montgomery and open a rooming house. And it was in Montgomery that Daddy met Rufe Payne, a black street singer known thereabouts as Tee-Tot. Tee-Tot taught Daddy to sing the blues, not just mimic a black man, but to reach out and touch that common pool of emotion.

Daddy debuted at a Montgomery amateur night when he was twelve years old, with a number called "The WPA Blues":

> I got a home in Montgomery
> A place I like to stay
> But I have to work for the WPA
> And I'm dissatisfied—I'm dissatisfied . . .

It won him $15.

From there he played the tonks, picking up experience and more than one scar. Those clubs along the Alabama-Tennessee border and on down through Alabama were (and still are) *mean*. Once Daddy had to club a guy with the stainless steel fret-bar from a steel guitar, which Daddy had observed worked very well as an argument settler. It would have worked for Daddy if the other fellow had followed the rules instead of raising up and taking a huge bite out of Hank Williams' eyebrow, hair and all.

By the time he was fifteen, Daddy was working pretty steady with a backup band he called the Drifting Cowboys. Lilly would come along to each show, handling the money before it disappeared into somebody else's pocket and seeing that everybody got paid and didn't lose too many instruments. His big break, though, came at a medicine show in Banks, Alabama, where he met the woman who was going to become my mother.

Audrey Sheppard was beautiful—long blond hair and a figure that could melt the wax off a Dixie Cup at fifty feet. And she had drive, something that Hank was sadly lacking. She took pity on the singing scarecrow, and in December of 1944 they were married.

And, darn it, she just *knew* that there was more to this Hank Williams than the Nickle-and-Dime Nightclub in West Nowhere, Alabama. She knew he was destined for great things, if he'd just get off his butt and *try*. And if he wouldn't try, well, she'd try for him.

Two years after they were married, she'd gotten him as far as Nashville, all the way to the studios of WSM Radio, the home of the Grand Ole Opry.

What they were to do in Nashville was to meet Fred Rose and his son, Wesley, the heads of the most powerful publishing concern in Nashville. Actually, the only game in town. Fred Rose had been a pretty good songwriter of the Tin Pan Alley variety when he decided to chuck it all and join hands with Roy Acuff, the grandest star of the Grand Ole Opry, to form Nashville's first publishing house, Acuff-Rose. It had been a smashing success, thanks to such writers as Pee Wee King, whose "Tennessee Waltz" remains one of the most recorded songs of all time.

Fred and Wesley ate lunch the same time every day, at a drugstore across the street from their offices. But before lunch, they played Ping-Pong at WSM, and it was during one of those Ping-Pong games that Mother approached them.

My husband, she told Fred Rose, writes songs, and we were wondering if you'd be interested in hearing a few.

It was a slow afternoon, and Fred and Wesley both said, why not? So they went to an unused studio in the radio station and had Daddy sing about six songs, including "When God Comes and Gathers His Jewels" and "Six More Miles to the Graveyard."

The Roses had been looking for some hard country songs for their latest singing sensation, Molly O'Day, and they were quick to sign Hank up and take a couple of his songs. That began one of the most productive relationships in the history of popular music.

Fred Rose was a master craftsman, and Hank Williams had all the raw material of genius, and the mesh was perfect from the start. Fred Rose took over the direction of Hank's career. He wangled him a recording contract with MGM, whose only other country act at the time was Bob Wills, directed Hank to head for Shreveport and join the Louisiana Hayride, second to the Opry in terms of prestige but much more open to a talented newcomer than the very conservative WSM show.

Most importantly, Fred Rose worked with Hank on his songwriting. Daddy was a brilliant but unpolished writer—songs came in scratched on the backs of envelopes or on random slips of paper. Sometimes there was a whole song, sometimes just a verse, sometimes just a few words that Daddy planned to work into a song later. Fred would work with each one of those snippets, changing each as little as possible in order to retain the flavor of Daddy's writing. On songs where he made major changes, such as "Mansion on the Hill" or "Kawliga" (it was Fred who suggested that the real Indian pining for his lost love in the song be changed to a wooden Indian, and that change made the song a huge hit), Fred took a by-line as coauthor.

Just as importantly, the Roses took direction of Hank's career (away from Mother, more or less). They had been looking for the country singer who could make the leap out of strictly "hillbilly" and into the mainstream of music, and they thought that Hank was that person.

Could that man perform! He had charisma, although you wouldn't know it from looking at his emaciated frame and balding head. Whether he was singing in Montgomery, Alabama, or the Amish country of Pennsylvania, he was absolutely riveting. You only had to hear him sing once to know you'd been in the presence of something very, very special.

At least, that's what I've been told, and the written records seem to bear that out. Imagine Elvis on stage, or the Beatles in their first American tour. *That* kind of electric reaction between audience and artist.

But there were demons in my father, and because of the way he was, or the people around him, or the temper of the times, they were demons he could never exorcize. He was practically an alcoholic by the time he was fifteen—necessary to survive the clubs he played, I think. Nowdays we call those places "toilets," and I guess I've played a few myself. He'd hurt his back early on, and the pain nagged at him for as long as he was alive. Sometimes he was able to drown it in liquor, and later on he found an easing in the pills. Or maybe he found an excuse for the liquor and the pills in his pain. Who's to say?

Daddy was haunted by his genius, and when the blues came around at midnight he had no place to turn, no one to grab ahold of. His life was marked by strong women, first Lilly, his mother, then Audrey, his wife, and I'd be lying if I didn't admit that they pushed. Lord, how they pushed!

Maybe he needed the pushing. There are questions I'd like to have discussed with him, answers I wished I knew. His relationship with my mother was stormy. She hated his drinking and belittled the fact that he could never be the person she thought he should be. They fought, bitterly and sometimes in public, but there was always a reconciliation at the end. That is, right up until the very end.

The problem was (I think) that despite the hangers-on, well-wishers, managers, wife, and what have you, nobody ever gave the slightest thought to helping Daddy cope with his success. He was successful beyond his wildest imagination, and that was the problem. Literally, beyond his wildest imagination, and he couldn't imagine what to do next.

On the balance, though, times were more private then than they are now, and Daddy guarded his privacy fanatically. No one would even *think* about telling him that he drank too much or he was ruining his career and his life. Maybe it's still the same way now—who counseled Elvis in his final days?

I was born May 26, 1949, in Shreveport, and the next month Daddy got his long awaited shot at the Grand Ole Opry. The Opry had been very leery of allowing him to perform, because they'd heard all the stories of his wild and wooly ways, but he had too many hit records to ignore.

The performance went down as one of the great moments in country music history, and he walked off the stage as the biggest star country music had ever known.

Three years later he was dead.

What happened was those demons caught up with him, hounded him, and finally ran him into the ground. He became a parody of himself, and his fans began coming to his concerts, perversely, to see if he could really stand on stage through the whole thing without falling off. Yet he did go on—the promoters *made* him go on. Whether the people were paying to see Hank Williams sing or to see him die a little bit on stage didn't make a damn bit of difference, as long as the people were paying.

In 1951 Daddy's "Cold, Cold Heart" became a million-selling pop hit for Tony Bennett.

The next year, Daddy was fired from the Grand Ole Opry and sent back in shame to the Louisiana Hayride in Shreveport.

The very promoters who'd forced him on stage refused to book him any longer, because he was a "drunk."

The top record of 1952 was Daddy's "Jambalaya."

Finally, even Mother had had enough, and she filed for divorce. Ever the businesswoman, she demanded—and got—fifty percent of the future royalties to his songs. Hank moved out of the house on Franklin Road and into an apartment with another aspiring singer named Ray Price. The divorce was final in May 1952, and even then he never stopped begging her to take him back.

Not even after he decided to get married again. He'd met Billie Jean Jones Eshlimar backstage while he was still at the Opry and Billie Jean was seeing Faron Young. Daddy proposed in the autumn, and he and Billie Jean were married not once, but *three* times: once by a justice of the peace in New Orleans, then twice on stage in Shreveport before the paying customers. Twice, because the first performance was sold out.

It was pathetic.

Daddy had gotten a good booking for New Year's day in Canton, Ohio, and he left early to drive through a blinding snowstorm that had blanketed Tennessee that weekend. Daddy had hired a driver named Charles Carr to drive him to Canton, and had talked him into stopping along the way for Daddy to get a shot of painkiller for his back. Carr began to worry that Hank was lying so quietly, and in Oak Hill, West Virginia, he stopped to check.

Daddy was dead.

The autopsy said heart failure linked to excessive drinking, and so it was.

His biggest song of 1953 was "I'll Never Get Out of This World Alive."

Mother claimed until the day she died that she and Hank had decided to get back together, just as soon as he got back from Ohio, and I'll always believe that.

Nashville was left in the lurch—what to do now that the legend was dead?

That question happened to coincide with the same question asked by my mother, and the answers came out the same. Nashville wholeheartedly adopted the Cult of Hank Williams, and the way Hank done it became, quite honestly, the only way to go.

To hear the tributes, one would think that the entire city took turns kissing Daddy while he was still alive. Everybody loved Hank. Everybody worried over his, ahem, "excesses." Everybody tried to help him.

While he was alive, he was despised and envied; after he died, he was some kind of saint. And that's exactly how Nashville decided to treat Daddy—country music's first authentic saint.

I was the chosen son.

But, underneath all the squeaky clean tributes and the "Hank Williams, bless his name" from the stage of the Grand Ole Opry, there was a whole other Hank Williams myth being born. It's a myth that I ran right smack into, and it changed my life.

Simply this: A lot of people were not nearly as blind as the powers-that-be in Nashville thought they were, and what they saw wasn't the same as what they heard described from the stage of the Grand Ole Opry. What they saw was a great man slipping into a maelstrom of drugs and liquor while his "friends" stood by, unwilling or unable to help. A whole new generation of singers and songwriters, inspired by the Hank Williams story, were trapped along the sidelines while every cliché in the book came true. Money couldn't buy happiness. Suffering led to flights of genius. Business success led to personal failure. He lived fast, died young, and left a beautiful corpse.

While the city boys mourned the passing of James Dean, the rebel without a cause, the country boys were mourning the death of their own rebel, and wondering about his causes. It was a time, in the early 1950s, of martyrs.

While the Opry was piously evoking Hank the Saint, Hank the Hellraiser was capturing the soul of country music. It's still that way today.

Gotta go down in flames? Gotta die young? Gotta drink till you can't stand on stage anymore? I've heard it all my life, folks, and I'm not buying any more.

There's a story Minnie Pearl told me once—she toured with Daddy quite a bit, especially toward the last—and that story still sends chills down my back. I tape recorded it once, so I would never forget it.

What she said was this:

"As I walked backstage, they were bringing Hank up the steps. He looked at me. I sound overdramatic when I tell it, but it was true—the look that he had on his face was of such pleading that I just never will forget it. He said, 'Minnie, I just can't work. I can't work, Minnie. Tell them I can't work!'

"Well, I didn't know what to do. I had no authority; I was paid just like everyone else. But they went ahead and made him work. It was bad. He sang maybe a couple of songs, then the promoter told me to stay with him between shows. He said, 'Minnie, he may listen to you. Maybe you can keep him from getting worse than he is.'

"This was between shows in San Diego, and we were driving around, trying to keep him from getting anything that would make him get in worse shape than he was, and trying to keep the crowd away from him. He would go with me, and he wouldn't go with anyone else. So we started singing. I remember his feet were big and his legs were so long, and he hunkered down in the car with his feet up, and he was looking out the side of the car, and he was singing 'I Saw the Light.' And then he stopped, and he turned around, and his face broke up, and he said, 'Minnie, I don't see no more light. Minnie, that's what's wrong. There ain't no light for me!'

"At that time Hank's life was a tunnel, the way he described it, and it was as if he was in a cage. If he could have seen one ray of light come in, we might have saved him."

Minnie was crying when she told this, and I think I was crying a little, too. All I could think of was, "Man, this woman is *serious*! That was the way it was." And it's still a horrible feeling, after all these years, and sometimes I want to throw out a life preserver, back through time, or try to give him the one ray of light that would have made all the difference.

8

I'll Think of Something

The doctors don't tell me that if I make it a week and a day, I'll live—no sir. They don't want to get my mind going on some downward spiral. They tell me that later, that your mind has so much to do with your physical being. They can only do so much, the doctors tell me, the rest is up to the Man Upstairs and my own will to live.

On the third day I ask for a little soup, which I get through my straw. It is, to the best of my knowledge, one of the best things I've ever tasted. Later, the nurses feed me a milk shake, and it is sublime.

On the fifth day I beg for a whirlpool bath. I keep telling them that I played football in high school and I know all about those strained muscles. If they think you can strain yourself playing football, for gosh sakes, they ought to try falling down a mountain! Parts of me hurt where I didn't even know I had parts. The doctors confer, and, lo and behold, I'm on my way to the whirlpool. Compared to the whirlpool, that bowl of soup was *nothing*. The water rushes around, and I feel my body, one muscle at a time, shouting its thanks. I feel human again.

Outside my door, though, there's a shitstorm going on, and Dick Willey, Bill Dyer, and J. R. Smith are doing their level best to keep their collective thumbs in the dike. People are pouring into Missoula—my mother is here, and she's a sick woman. Gwen is here, and she's all the time coming into my room and telling me she loves me, that she was wrong about everything, that if I can just keep from dying, everything will be all right. Great. Just what a sick man needs. Gwen and my mother hate each other. Gwen has a friend with her. Lots of things I'd rather not have had on my mind.

My real friends do a great job, and they're there every day. Betty Willey spends a lot of time by my bed, and just having her around cheers me up. "Boy, I don't know what it is," she says, "but you're left here for some reason."

Johnny Cash and June Carter come to my bedside, and they've seen hard times before, and they're strong.

Merle Kilgore comes, and when he comes into the Intensive Care Unit, I can see his hands are shaking, and I swear he looks like he's been crying. I can't believe it—old Merle had even been touring with me before the fall, and he's not one to cry.

"Hank," he says, the gravel voice quivering. "Hank, please think about my job before you *ever* do anything like this again!"

If it's possible to break up laughing when you're totally wired into machines, I came real close.

The people who come to Missoula are shocked, but Merle and Dick and Johnny and Bill manage to condition most of them before they come into the room. The only way to recognize me, they tell the new visitors, is by my hands, because they're the only things that haven't changed. My weight has dropped to about 165 in a matter of days. My head is all swollen, covered with bandages. I'm still wearing my rings, though. When the people come into my room, there's varying looks of happiness and sorrow. Some cry, and I do my best to comfort them.

On the sixth day things have sort of settled into a routine. The doctors come in the morning, take my chart out, look at it and go, "Um . . . um-huh . . . ," check me over, and give me a shot of Demerol, which is synthetic morphine. It feels better than anything I've ever done, and I like it. Johnny Cash is sitting in my room, and he watches me very closely.

"Ole Demerol's pretty good, ain't it, Hank?" Johnny says, catching me pretty much off guard.

"Yea, pretty good," I say. All I've got to do is push the button to call the nurse, who'll give me a shot. Pretty good.

"Believe me, bennies and all that, they're nothing compared to this. This is the big one, so don't go pushin' the ole button if you don't need it."

I think about that a lot, 'cause I figure Johnny Cash knows what he's talking about. It'd be real easy, I think, to just sink back and let that needle wash away all the pain. I think about Cash, the needle, and my time up on the mountain, and after that I don't push the button too much.

Every morning at ten I get to go to the whirlpool, and that's pretty much the high point of my life—I'm also falling in love with the nurse, but I guess that's to be expected. I mean how can you *help* falling in love with at least a few of 'em, when they're helping you wash up and cleaning your scars with this little foam rubber thing that felt *sooo* good and shaving you wherever you needed to be shaved, which was just about everyplace. Yea, it's love.

The whirlpool is good—I just stand and stare at that stainless steel tank while the nurses undress me. Then they lower me in and I rest my head on the foam rubber pad. It helps clear my head, makes the drug-induced, fall-induced hallucinations go away for a little while. I don't see snakes all over the floor while I'm in the whirlpool. I don't suddenly wake up and panic and wonder where I am when I'm there.

Inside my head I am healing. My brain is playing me like a fish on a line–each day, it gives me a little more leeway. It protects me from depression better than any of the doctors' drugs, potent though they are. I am healing inside, and I think my mind is trying

69

to save what it learned up there on old Ajax. In some odd way, I feel secure.

On the eighth day I am not dead. Instead, I'm in the whirlpool, and it's wonderful, as usual. I'm lounging there when someone comes into the room with a guitar.

A guitar.

It scares me, like no animal I've ever hunted in the wilds of Africa has ever scared me. It scares me down deep in the pit of my stomach. It is reality intruding on my cozy little world in the whirlpool bath, with my loving nurses in attendance. It's an intrusion I don't want.

At first I ignore it. I lean back on the foam rubber pad and let the whirlpool take hold of my body and wash my cares away, twang, twang. I close my eyes and try to sink back into my reverie, but the guitar doesn't go away. It stays there, an image on the back of my closed eyelids, six strings and a bunch of cheap wood intent on ruining my perfect morning.

In disgust I open my eyes and look at the damn thing. I fancy it's staring back at me—taunting me, in fact. Having a good laugh on ole Hank Williams Junior, who's setting naked in a puddle of swirling water, staring like some trapped animal. Yep, it's definitely staring at me, and there's no sense in staying in this bath another minute longer. I signal my loving nurses, and I'm out, getting all dried off while the guitar chuckles on.

Guitars are like that, you know. You're just a little kid, and somebody puts a guitar in your hand, and before you can even say *twang*, you're hooked. You work your ass off until you get pretty good, and maybe you keep on working until you get great. Or maybe, if you're like a certain kid I know very, very well, you get almost good and you figure that'll get you by. After all, if you've got the Williams name behind you, it didn't matter whether you could play a killer guitar or not, see. All you had to do was walk out there on stage—you could be carrying a fifty-pound sack of potatoes, it really didn't matter—and they'd go wild over you. Plumb crazy. If you carried a guitar, well that was just icing on the cake.

I think this ole guitar knows all that.

But my mind plays out a little more string, and I can do anything I want to do, right? Right?

I sit down, and some guy hands me the guitar, which at least isn't smirking anymore. It's very light, a cheap little Spanish gut-string guitar, and my fingers run over the strings, up the frets. They touch a string, and there's a flash in my mind.

My fingers remember!

They remember!

The rehabilitation room is very quiet. There are several people around me, and they're watching closely. There is a knot in my stomach, but I feel it fading as my fingers slide up and down the fret and pick out their own tune.

The tune they pick is Mason Williams' "Classical Gas."

It rolls off maybe a little slow, my ears inform me, but otherwise just fine.

I am so happy!

The audience is smiling, maybe they're even applauding, I don't know.

All I know is that I can still play, and until this moment I didn't realize exactly what that meant to me. As long as I can play, I can be a part of music. I know I'll never sing again—my face is shattered and I can live with that, so thank you, Lord, for leaving me my hands!

I go straight into a Chet Atkins' style rendition of "Freight Train," then roar into Doc Watson's "Deep River Blues." The little guitar is singing happily and it's not even smirking. I have taken a step into the real world, and I am still on my feet. Damn it all, I feel great!

I'm still in a happy trance while they're wheeling me back to my room, but typical of these sorts of things, I have to go to the bathroom. They wheel me up to the bathroom door—I can sort of hobble like an old man, holding on tightly to whatever I could find—and I open the door and there's a mirror on the wall.

There are no mirrors in the bathroom in my room.

71

There are no mirrors in my room at all.

Now I know why. There is a monster looking out from that mirror at me, and I have a sick feeling that I know who the monster is.

"Hello, sweets," I say to the monster.

You know, I feel pretty good (I tell myself). I thought I was getting well fast. What a surprise.

I look like a pale watermelon with a side of it caved in. My head is swollen and long. My right cheek is all pulled up, funny like, and it twitches. My left eye doesn't move. My right eye is all purple, sickly purple. No teeth, and my jaw—such as it is—is wired up. Lots of stitches up the side of the face. Ribs sticking out. Buttocks and thighs just like the old man I hobble around like. No muscles anywhere.

I don't have to go to the bathroom anymore. I stare for a long time, trying to get used to the monster, then I sit back in my chair and ask to be taken to my room.

What do I do now? No more social life, that's for sure. Can you imagine the kind of woman who'd want to spend the rest of her life with somebody who looked like me? There's not that much money in the world! And entertaining? Out of the question, boy. Can you imagine people paying money to see somebody who looks like you, even if he's the greatest guitar player in the universe?

"Well, Lord," I think. "What's it going to be?"

Then again, I think I'll go into forestry. That would be very nice, since I'd probably get to live up in the mountains. I could be a hermit.

I wouldn't be the first person who had to live without a social life—no, let's be honest about this thing. What I mean is there's not going to be any more sex life. No more women.

That's it.

Well, I suppose it could be worse.

I play the guitar every day, and I think I'm getting better.

Yea, it could *definitely* be worse!

9

"Just a Normal Abnormal Childhood"

Let me read you a letter from my mother, Audrey. The letter wasn't to me—it was to my father, Hank Senior, and he'd been dead for two years. It was a letter for the fan club, I guess, on the occasion of Daddy's birthday:

DEAREST HANK

It's your birthday again and that means it's time for our big Hank Williams Day in Montgomery, Ala. . . . . Everybody is just so wonderful to take time out from their busy schedules to come and join in and be with us for your day. Oh, how the people loved you, Hank. They still do and will for now and always. I'm sure you must know but I want to tell you how the people in Mont. went all out for your day last Sept. They worked hard to make it the biggest event that had ever been in their city. I'm happy to say, they were very successful. They have already begun to make plans for this year's festivities.

As the entertainers gather from all four corners they talk of the genius that you were and of what great showmanship you had. Speaking of your work you know you've just had a new record released which looks very big. I saw the write up on it in [*Bill-*

73

board Magazine] today and it was good. TEARDROP ON A ROSE and ALONE AND FORSAKEN. I was in New York last week to see Mr. Walker [of MGM Records] and he really likes TEARDROP ON A ROSE. I'm so thrilled because he's going to let me do the poem about Hank, Jr. (Little Bocephus, as you called him) which you wrote. I know I can't do it justice but I'll do my best and I hope the people will like it. . . .

Honey, the children have grown so much. Lycrecia is a lovely sweet girl and does a good job when it comes to singing. She is now 13. Little Bocephus is a prince of a little guy and every day in every way he looks more like you. I know that makes you happy. Me too. Oh and what a voice he has. One of these days before too long he'll be singing for you. . . .

Before I go I want to ask you to give our kindest regards to Mommie Williams.

Take care and help guide us right.

Your family sends their love,

AUDREY, LYCRECIA AND HANK, JR.

Actually, I didn't look like Daddy at all. At least, I didn't think I looked like Daddy, but the memories are all jumbled up.

The memories begin around the time of the letter, when I was about five years old. Daddy was dead, but I didn't really *remember* that. What I remember, though, is good times. See, I was Hank Williams' son, and I lived in Hank Williams' house, and Hank Williams' wife was my mother. And let me tell you something—for a little kid, all that was neat.

Mother gave parties, and they all seem to run together into one long party. There was always a party going on, and there were always people who wanted to come to Hank Williams' house. Later, it dawned on me that a lot of people were interested in seeing Hank Williams' widow: Mother was a striking woman, blond and beautiful and totally charged with energy. For a long time I thought she was a princess. But there were always parties going in the house on Franklin Road in Nashville, with its heart-shaped headboards and heart-shaped bathtubs with gold fixtures. There were parties, and, usually, I was the center attraction.

74

Imagine people like Jerry Lee Lewis and Perry Como, Ray Charles and Brenda Lee, Red Foley and Johnny Cash—everybody from the Grand Ole Opry at one time or another—Sam Phillips from Sun Records, all the greats in the music industry, they all came to Hank Williams' house, and they all took time out to talk to me and maybe give me a few pointers on the guitar or piano.

In fact, they *loved* to give me a few pointers, helping Hank Williams' kid make it to the stage—but I'm getting ahead of myself again.

What was I like when I was five? Spoiled, I think. I knew that the people who came to Mother's parties were important in some way or the other. I knew they were big-shot grownups, and all they could do was tell me how good I was, how smart I was, how much I looked like Daddy and what a great man he was. What was I supposed to think?

Yea, I guess I was a little show-off.

And I learned to idolize my father. At first, I thought he was like a president or king or something, like any five- or six-year-old would think. He was just a real famous guy, and that was all there was to it. His memories were all over the place. His old trailer that he used to haul around on the road was parked out back. His guitars were scattered all around the house, and people would come in and pick them up, reverently like, like there was still some of that old Williams magic in them. Maybe there was. I knew where Mother kept some of Daddy's guns, and when I got a little older I'd sneak in and look at them. Somethimes I'd even sneak in a friend or two to show them off.

Daddy's music was always getting played around the house. New records were constantly getting released.

There were times, I remember, when I was sure that Daddy wasn't dead at all; that any minute he was going to step from behind the barn or out of some closet and say, "Bo-Cephus, watcha up to, son?" or just give me holy hell about picking up his guitars or his guns. I think I spent a few years looking over my shoulder, but Daddy didn't show up.

I can't put my finger on the first time I realized it, but deep down inside there was always a feeling that something was expected of me. Maybe Mother whispered in my ear while I was still in the cradle, I don't know.

I knew what I had to do, and I know that sounds pretty silly. But, understand, it wasn't like I could sit down when I was five years old and articulate what I was going to do with the rest of my life, thank you, and watch for my first record. But—and it's kind of hard to explain—other kids could play cowboys and Indians and imagine that they'd grow up to be cowboys. I couldn't do that. I knew that I would never grow up to be a cowboy or a fireman or the president of the United States. I knew I'd grow up to be a singer.

That's all there ever was, the only option from the beginning.

When there are never any other options, you don't spend your childhood sulking, either. I couldn't imagine, with my childhood imagination, not wanting to follow in my father's footsteps. I almost couldn't wait to get on stage—I swear it was bred into me! I knew it because there was nothing else I could think of to do, and I knew it because my mother and everybody else told me that's what I'd do.

Probably a few words more about my mother wouldn't hurt, because Mother was a force to be reckoned with in her own right. I love my mother now, but there was a time when I hated her as fully as an adolescent is capable of hating. Maybe all adolescents hate their mother at one point or another. I hated her because maybe she whispered in my ear when I was a baby, and I hated her because I couldn't dream of anything else but the stage. I hated her for a lot of grown-up reasons as well, but the bottom line is those dreams I couldn't have.

See, my mother was a complex, troubled woman, and more than anything else, *she believed* in the glamour of the country music business. She believed that there was a place for her in the music business, and that it was her rightful place not only as the widow of Hank Williams, but as a personality in her own right.

She'd been a star—well, at least she'd been able to bask in the reflected glory of my father. She'd been in his band, sure, and she'd cut some records, but I don't think I'd be betraying her memory if I told you she just plain couldn't sing. But she knew the stage, I'll tell you that. She had charisma. But she couldn't sing. At least, not enough to make her the Next Big Thing in Nashville. A couple of critics have compared her voice to fingers scraping across a chalkboard. Maybe that's a little off, but not by much.

After Daddy died, Mother was faced with a dilemma: How could she remain a part of the business she loved? How could she guarantee her place in country music now that Hank Williams was dead?

Perhaps I'm being too heartless and perhaps I'm looking back through a fog of years. But the parties started, and the people came to Hank Williams' house to meet with Hank Williams' widow and play with Hank Williams' son.

There's even a school of thought that holds that my mother was broke, that there was nothing of consequence in the Williams estate, and more than anything else she sought to increase the value of Hank's music. There are people who say that, after Daddy died, Mother began a coldly calculated campaign to fan the flames of the Hank Williams myth to guarantee the financial security of herself and her children. Nobody wanted to record Hank Williams' songs, and Mother set about to change that. Nope.

Mother had all the money she'd ever need for the rest of her life. The foreign royalties alone would have seen to that. She didn't have to throw herself headfirst into the business of country music. She didn't have to have parties every night, or try to cut records of her own, or organize tours. She didn't have to make me a reincarnation of my father.

I didn't think about that until much later, and I held it against her for a long time. But more about that later.

There was a good side that worried about her children and what this life was doing to them. One side of her wanted to keep me away from the music business for as long as possible—made it real tough, for example, for me to get my first guitar. Every time I asked for a guitar of my own, she'd answer with something like, "Aw, Hank, you don't need a guitar." Drove me crazy for a while until I squealed enough to get a cutdown Gibson of my very own. Mother seemed caught between those two poles: I think it eventually pulled her apart.

As for me, when I was eight years old I played my first show in the thriving metropolis of Swainsboro, Georgia, on some tiny stage, and I was pretty funny. I walked out on that stage with my hands stuffed into the pockets of my little black suit, with my hair all slicked back, and I sang "Lovesick Blues" in my little eight-year-old voice. The audience *looooved* it! They went crazy, shouting about "Hank's little boy" this and "Hank's little boy" that! that I just stood there with my hands in my pockets, and I wasn't even a little bit afraid. "This is it," I thought. "This is what I have to do, and an awful lot is expected of me." Mother was both proud and scared, and the next day after the show I was back at school, playing baseball at recess and joking around with my friends. Even then, there were two clear-cut worlds, and I lived in both of them.

We did about ten dates the year I was eight, mostly with Mother and her act, my half-sister Lycrecia, who was a damn good singer, and a couple of Opry icons: Ernest Tubb and Grandpa Jones. I don't know how old ET and Grandpa Jones felt about having a kid open the show, but they treated me very well, although now I figure Audrey would have ripped their throats out if they'd said a cross word to me. Every show was the same: I could have done anything, and the crowd would have gone wild.

My voice—imagine how my voice sounded, eight years old and trying to hit those high notes, trying to break into a yodel. God, it was awful!

The crowd kept going crazy. I couldn't do any wrong on a bet. Just standing out there in my black suit with my hands in my pockets, sounding just like a little boy and watching the people scream. Now, it seems almost eerie. Then, it seemed like the most natural

78

thing in the world. No different from going to school and learning cursive writing. No different from reading, writing, and 'rithmetic. Stage presence, delivery, and style.

That first year I didn't miss a day of school. The next year, when I was nine, we upped it to twenty dates, and that summer I went on the road in earnest with Mother's Caravan of Stars. Mother had just staged a much-publicized national talent search, and we got great press in Nashville:

"I've been sort of holding Lycrecia and Hank back," Audrey said [to Nashville reporter Bill Maples]. "I wanted them to get an education."

"Phooey to an education," said young Hank.

"Show business can ruin an adult, much less a child. I wanted them to really get their feet on the ground," Audrey continued.

Hank Jr., who's at Robertson Academy, is a baseball fan and likes skin diving. . . . We listened to Hank Jr. sing some of the songs which made his dad so famous. The similarity of style is haunting. He has the same lonesome quality, the same break in his voice, the same pronunciation.

"How much will the tour make?" [Maples asked].

"I'm afraid to say how much," Audrey said, "but we've been getting requests from people to appear in their towns, so I'm encouraged about it."

"Speaking of money, people talk a lot these days about how much you're making from Hank's songs. Can you tell me how much that is?"

"I'd rather not say how much," Audrey said. "But I will say that every time I get a royalty check, I'm amazed."

There's even a picture of me in the paper, looking for all the world like a normal nine-year-old kid. Fat chance.

It was like that—a steady stream of music people, music lives, and music business in and out of the house. School on weekdays and the road on weekends. And it was a very big, very classy world for a little kid. I think the kids at school were in awe of me; I played on that every so often. Kids are that way, I guess.

One thing stands out, though, and I don't think I'll ever forget it. I was watching Mother on television once; one of those local, syndicated country music television shows out of Nashville, and she forgot the words to one of her songs.

Just forgot the words, that's all.

After the show she called the house, and when I talked to her, I think she was crying. I felt so sad for her because she forgot the words. She was like a saint to me or something. As far as the music business went, she had been through it all. She was the one who directed me, who told me what I needed to do and who I needed to meet. And she forgot the words.

So the fifties fed into the sixties. I practiced my guitar and my piano and I got pretty good. Mostly I practiced rock and roll, because when I turned on the radio that was what I was listening to. Elvis and Chuck Berry. Ray Charles and Chubby Checker. I practiced those rock and roll licks, and I worked at singing those rock and roll songs—to myself, to my friends. If I'd gone on stage and sung "Roll Over Beethoven," I was convinced that my fans would have lynched me, right then and there. Maybe worse.

So on weekends I sang Hank Williams, and on weekdays I practiced rock and roll. Mother worked with me on stage patter—that was the secret of my daddy, she said. He could communicate with the common people. He could laugh and tell jokes on stage and be relaxed, and I needed to learn to be the same way. So we practiced telling jokes, and we practiced our stage manners. The hard part was relaxing—I was, hell, I still am—shy. It was hard for me to meet people, and when I went on stage that tenseness translated to the audience.

I learned my father's mannerisms, and I worked on his voice. I practiced in front of the mirror until I had them down pat. I was good and I knew it.

People would come over, and I'd go get my own guitar and sing a few songs and they were knocked out! Stunned. They were professional entertainers, some of these people, and they remembered a little kid who was too much of a show-off. Or they remembered Mother's incessant harangues about "Hank Williams' only son." I don't think they expected me to have a shred of talent of my own.

But when they heard me play, I don't think they could believe it.

80

He really *is* just like Hank, they said. His hands are the same. He's such a little old guy. Boy, he sounds older or he looks younger than he is.

The people who came over to my mother's house were my toughest audience because they were the best in the business. By the time I was thirteen, I'd made believers of them, too, and I was ready to become a star.

It was, after all, my birthright.

I thought.

10

Hank Williams Had a Son; Son Sings

That's my favorite newspaper title—"Hank Williams Had a Son; Son Sings"—it's from Dallas or Fort Worth or some other place in Texas, and it appeared when I was fourteen years old. The writer also predicted that at the rate I was going I might soon be just as big a star as my daddy.

And boy, didn't I know it!

I'd premiered at the Grand Ole Opry at the age of eleven, and I guess it just wasn't as scary as I thought it would be. I mean, I was scared—who wouldn't be? This was where my father made it, after all. His first appearance on the Grand Ole Opry has passed into the permanent lore of country music. Daddy was twenty-five and unknown, and the Opry at that time was mainly interested in the heavyweights. And it had them to spare—Roy Acuff, Minnie Pearl, Red Foley, just to name a few. But there was my daddy, and not too many people applauded when he took the stage. But by the time he'd finished "I got a feelin' called the blu-oo-oo-oo-oo-ues . . ." you'd better believe they were applauding. You'd better believe they were plumb out of their minds!

83

Seven encores he did, and when he walked off that stage he was a superstar.

It's like something Elvis Presley told me, a long time after I walked out on that stage. I was in Hollywood making a movie, *A Time to Sing*, and Elvis happened to drop by the set.

"Hank," he said, "I just want to tell you that your daddy was really something, man."

There were just a few of us there, and Elvis was already so big that he couldn't walk down the street without starting a riot.

"I want you to know," Elvis was saying, "that I thought about Hank when I walked out on that Opry stage for the first time. All I could think about then was, 'This is the same stage Hank Williams was on, and now I'm here.'"

Maybe it's ironic that after that first appearance the head of the Opry suggested that Elvis try to find a day job, and that Elvis cried all the way back to Memphis after the Opry show. Then he went on to become the biggest star since Hank Williams. There's some kind of justice in that, I think.

But I didn't have those kinds of problems, at least, not my first time at the Opry.

This was at the old Ryman Auditorium, not the new multimillion-dollar Opry House at the Opryland Amusement Park. The Ryman was sort of a falling-down gospel-preachin' auditorium—a place that could keep a ghost or two without seriously disturbing the operation. The dressing rooms were the size of postage stamps, and I was back in one of them rehearsing with Faron Young, who once told Mother I couldn't sing a lick. She almost killed him on the spot. Faron was always a joker.

Mother came running back to the dressing room, and she was white as a sheet.

"You've gotta go on!" she said. "They gave you the wrong time, and you've got to go on right now!"

They had given me ten extra minutes, but everything had gotten mixed up and I had to go on right away—they were even announcing my name to the audience. To tell the truth, if I'd been as scared

84

as Mother, I don't think I could have gone on at all. I just picked up my guitar and walked with Mother to the stage. I was ready to play, and I was calm. Honest—I just wasn't that nervous. I'd been brought up to be a singer, and I was getting ready to practice what I'd been taught all my life. I walked out across those boards that my daddy walked on and was introduced. Then I sang:

> I got a feelin' called the blu-oo-oo-oo-ues,
>   oh lawd
> Since my baby said goodbye.
> Lawd, I don't know what I'll do
> All I do is sit and sigh . . .

I got about as far as "I got a feelin'," maybe not even that far, before the place went wild. People were on their feet, screaming and applauding, and I thought some of the women were going to pass out cold. I loved it, and I really tore into that song. All eleven-years-old of me.

> That last long day she said goodbye
> Well lawd, I thought I would cry
> She'd do me
> She'd do you
> She's got that kind of lovin'. . .

I kept it close to Daddy's version, but I tried to put a little rock and roll in there, and it worked like a charm. By the end of the song, right when I got to "I'm lo-oo-oo-nesome, I got the lovesick blues!", the crowd was screaming for more. And I was heading off stage, grinning like the cat that just got the canary. Mother was applauding. Everybody backstage was applauding. Even Faron looked reasonably happy, and I was just so proud I thought I was going to burst.

They called me back for an encore—which is *still* a rare occasion—and it was one of the happiest moments I remember.

The next weeks the papers were full of how I stole the show at the Opry, just like my daddy.

* * *

But I wasn't a star; not really. At least, I could see a difference. I was a novelty act, a singing bear or somebody who could juggle a hundred spoons. I knew I was close. Mother knew I was close. So we pushed together.

What I did was practice. I worked hard at learning my jokes and my funny stories. I listened to Daddy sing on records and tapes over and over again, then I'd practice myself, singing those songs until I had them letter perfect, mannerism for mannerism. Our voices *were* a lot alike, my father's and mine, and when I knew all the vocal tricks and all the inflections, I sounded a heck of a lot like Hank Williams.

What I needed was a legendary performance of my own.

That came in Detroit when I was fourteen, at a place called Cobo Hall. Detroit is a great city for country music because of the huge number of expatriate Southerners who live there. In a lot of ways it's even better than playing a big city in the South. In Detroit they're mighty happy just to see you. I'd been touring more and more, on the road with my mother's Caravan of Stars, and I'd gotten a little cocky. Night after night we were knocking them dead. Whether we were with Faron Young or Merle Kilgore or whoever, I just came out there on stage and blew them away—standing ovations every night.

The fame was having an effect on me in two directions. One side of me was eating it up. Here I was in my early teens, still just a kid, and people loved me. It was like being able to do no wrong. Oh, sure, I had my share of little heartbreaks and pouts, but come the weekend, I'd go out there on that stage and it would seem like the whole world was there for my asking.

The other side of the coin was a shy adolescent who hated to meet people face to face; whose best friends were ten or twenty years older than he was; who wondered, once in a rare while, what it would be like to be *normal* for a change. I don't think I smiled very much in those years. There were just too many things to worry about. Did I sound enough like Daddy on stage? Did I have those jokes just right? How was Mother doing; was she happy; did she think I was working hard enough? *Was* I working hard enough?

How could I smile? Music was a life's work for me, and I don't think I had time for too much other living. I have an interview I did when I was thirteen, just before the show in Cobo Hall, and it may be the only derogatory story written about me during those years. In fact, I didn't see the story until years later: I think Mother kept it from me. What the interviewer says is, "One gets the impression that Hank Williams Junior doesn't enjoy what he does very much." I'm really surprised that such a thing even got written—all the other interviewers said I was quiet, intelligent, and studious, working hard to perfect my art. It's hard to believe that one guy hit it so close.

Can you really enjoy something that you were raised believing you had to do? You can do it, and you can get a certain amount of pleasure from doing it, but it's not the same as choosing a path and sticking to it until you succeed. But the stage provided relief—I could get out there on stage and do anything, and they still loved me. And that made me happy. My voice was changing even, and one day I'd sing high, the next day low, and, boy, even that didn't matter! I could walk out there on stage and feel a wave of solid love wash over me from the audience.

The Detroit show was a huge package show, featuring just about every performer in Nashville, from Marty Robbins to Minnie Pearl. Red Foley was the emcee, just like when Daddy first appeared on the Opry, and I was ready.

"Ladies and gentlemen, presenting, direct from the Grand Ole Opry in Nashville, Tennessee, HANK WILLIAMS JUNIOR!"

One more deep breath, and I was out on that stage. There must have been 20,000 people out there, and the rumble started before I'd taken two steps.

> She's lo-o-o-o-ng gone . . .
> And now I'm lo-oo-oo-oo-oo-nesome blues . . .

Everything else had just been a prelude for this. I had that audience in the palm of my hand, dancing every time I hit one of those

"OO-OO-OO-OO's." I was *testifying*, Lord; I was preachin' the gospel of Hank Williams, and I'd just made about 20,000 converts! This was it—I knew it in my heart and I heard it in my voice. This was the one that was going to do it once and for all.

> I went down to the river to watch the
>   fish swim by
> But I got to the river so lonesome I
>   wanted to die
> Oh Lawwwwwwwwwwwd!
> Then I jumped in the river, but the dog-
>   goned river was dry.
> Got dem gone but not forgotten blu-oo-oo-oo-oo-ses!

You talk about crazy audiences, those Detroit folks went nuts, and the ovation went on for what seemed like forever. I was happy; boy, was I happy! I did three encores and I'll tell you this: I walked on that stage as a novelty; I walked off that stage as a star. You could feel it backstage, and the reactions were mixed. Minnie Pearl was beaming, because she loved my father and wished me only the best. Some of the other Nashville stars were not so happy. Don't believe all that stuff about Nashville being one big happy family. It isn't now and it wasn't then. Some of the big stars at the time, like Marty Robbins or Sonny James or Charley Pride, were not so happy about having me out there knocking them dead, especially knocking them them dead with Daddy's songs. They knew there would be no competing with Hank Williams. Hank Williams was a saint, and I was his chosen son.

Red Foley was pale, almost shaking, and I wondered what had happened to him to shake him up that badly. Later they told me that when I took the stage and launched into "Long Gone Lonesome Blues" Red told the people backstage, "I thought I heard a ghost. I thought for a second that was Hank out there!"

Audrey was scared, as scared as she'd ever been, I think. She was finally close to her goal, creating the second superstar. The closer she got to that goal, the more scared she got. At least, that's the only way I can explain her reticence. She'd been pushing hard for years and years, and now, all of a sudden, with the end nearly in sight, she seemed to be backing off. There was more and more talk of my being sure I wanted to go into show business, which was really a joke. There was more talk of letting me decide for myself what I wanted to do with my life. She even told the Nashville paper something very strange on the eve of one of my most important days: "Hank's mother said that she felt even though her son is talented in many ways, the greatest appeal [of me] is in the mannerisms, looks and treatment of a song that so greatly resembles the Hank Williams the nation loved."

The next night I made my first appearance on Ed Sullivan's television show. Fourteen was turning out to be one heck of a year.

Colonel Tom Parker set up the Ed Sullivan deal, and that's how Ed Sullivan introduced me. "Colonel Parker, who, of course, got us together with Elvis [pause for screaming], sent this young man up here to sing for us. His father was a famous singer in his own right. Hank Williams Junior, let's hear it for him!"

I looked hot, decked out in a big glittering Nudie suit, just like the best of those country music singers, and carrying a special Gibson Dove guitar. I did a couple of Daddy's songs—"Long Gone Lonesome Blues," which by now I was getting pretty good at, was the ringer, and the little girls screamed for me almost as much as they screamed for Elvis. Ole Ed was beaming like a happy father, and when I finished, they couldn't wait to ask me back.

Colonel Tom said I'd never be as big as Elvis, but that I had "all the stuff from which headliners are built. Hank Williams Junior could be the next BIG teen star."

National television and the biggest, most important man in the music business singing my praises—what else could you ask for?

Well, I'll tell you. In December 1963, I signed a deal with MGM Records—the company my father's royalties had built—guaranteeing me $300,000 a year. I also signed with the prestigious booking agency William Morris for personal appearances.

My first record was "Long Gone Lonesome Blues," and it was a hit.

11

Standing in the Shadows

I felt that old Silver Eagle bus eating up the highway on the way back to Nashville, and I knew, deep down inside, that this was *it*, the way things were supposed to be. I stretched out on my bunk in the back of the bus—my bus—and chuckled a little to myself. The luxury, the sheer, unadulterated luxury, of being able to stretch out was almost too much to bear. Now I had my bus, with my name painted on the side and everything, a home on the road instead of being packed into somebody's car along with the bass and the steel guitar.

I was a star. And stars should have their own buses. That was the way it worked.

And it was a darn sight better than the way I had been touring since I was eight. I stretched out in that bunk with the radio playing "I Wanna Hold Your Hand" and all I could think of was climbing up in the rear window of Mother's Cadillac and trying to get some sleep. I must've been around nine years old—so very long ago—and we were on our way back to Nashville from some show, maybe along this very highway. Everybody thought it was so funny watching little Hank climb up there, curl up into a little ball, and go to sleep. They all told me what a little trouper I was.

The rhythm of the new bus was seductive, and it was easy to lie in that bunk and remember. There were always too many of us for the car, no matter which car we took. Maybe it was Mother's Cadillac, or one of the band's old Pontiacs. Just so it would roll down the road. And come Friday afternoon, we'd start piling all the junk in the world into it. First we'd hook up this old trailer and fill it with as much stuff as we could stuff into it. The instruments, the PA system—it seemed to fill up real fast. What was left, we tied to the top of the car, until we looked more like an Okie family heading out of the dustbowl rather than a country band heading for a one-night stand.

That old stand-up bass always seemed to be left over, though—there just isn't much you can do with five feet of bass fiddle. So that went in the car, right down the middle.

Then we all piled in—me, Howard White, Buddy Spicher, Dale Potter, Willie Ackerman, Pete Drake, Ken Marvin, sometimes a comedian to open the show—and off we'd go, to exotic places like Knoxville or Shreveport or Macon. Once we'd get rolling, I'd climb up under the window, up where the radio speakers were, and go to sleep.

Except when I had to go to the bathroom. No more though—when I have to go to the bathroom now, all I've got to do is get up and go. I don't have to beg Buddy or Pete to *please* stop the car and let me out for just a *minute*. Or sometimes just keep my mouth shut until somebody stopped for a Coke, then hop out of the car real fast. The band always got a big kick out of that.

Mostly, they'd just talk. About the old days, sometimes about Daddy, always about either the business or women. That's what fuels men on the road still: the idea that tomorrow they're all either going to be stars or get laid. I just kept my mouth shut, and the talk flowed around me like water. Big words; dirty words; jokes; deals, and I remember wondering what all those words meant.

Sometimes they'd have a pint they'd be passing around, and

once one of them asked if maybe I'd like a little drink. That was a really big deal then. So they poured about three drops of whiskey into a glass, dumped in a little Coke, and handed it over. I drank it, real solemn-like, because it was important. They all laughed and laughed.

"Lookie-there," someone said. "Ain't he just like his old man? Little Hank's gonna tie one on!"

My face turned red, lying there on my bunk in the bus, and I was glad everyone else was up front. I could still taste that whiskey, and it still burned. And my face turned even redder, because after we had a drink they told me a joke.

"Listen to this, Little Hank," one of the band members said. "This'll kill ya: Ten toes up; ten toes down; two big asses going round and round . . ."

Everybody laughed, and I laughed, too. They just rolled, and I figured it must have been just about the funniest joke anyone ever told. So I got home, and the next morning I couldn't wait to tell our maid, Flossie, and Miss Audrey Ragland, who was sort of our housekeeper, my nannie, and general keeper-of-the-order. I lined them both up, told them the joke as best I could, and neither of them laughed. "Oh God," I thought. "I'm so embarrassed." I still can't face Flossie or Miss Ragland without blushing.

The bus rolled on, and the radio was playing Chuck Berry. I loved rock and roll. That used to make the band madder than hell, when I'd reach up over the front seat and start tuning the radio, looking for WLAC or some other big rock station. "Nigger music," they'd say. And I knew when they said it they didn't believe it for a minute. It used to come to a head when we were coming home from a show on Saturday night. Saturday night was Opry night, the Grand Ole Opry live from Nashville, Tennessee. You could pick it up almost anywhere in the South, and every Saturday night, without fail, someone from the band would tune in WSM, and there'd be the Opry. But I was still way too young for country music. I wanted to hear that rock and roll so I could sit in the back seat and sing along with Chuck Berry and with Jerry Lee Lewis. So we'd carry on and carry on about who was gonna listen to what, and that'd last until we got to Nashville or until I went to sleep. I usually went to sleep.

It's funny, I thought, but maybe not that much has changed. The bus is fancier, sure. But I remember that before I went to sleep each night, my last thoughts always seemed to be that, well, I guess this was how Daddy did it. He probably rode all cramped up in some car carrying on with his band just like I'm doing. That always made me feel good.

The bus rolled on through the Tennessee evening, and I thought about those early days on the road. Then I thought about Daddy, and how the audience was at the last town I played. Up front, I could hear Mother talking to someone, and the band was neck-deep into a poker game. It was almost like I wasn't even there.

And I had to write something. Just like that, it came on in a wave. I had to write something, because I could feel it boiling up inside me, something trying to get out.

"Daddy must have felt this way," I thought for a second, and then I felt the color go to my face again. "He might have felt this way, but I'd better not kid myself about what kind of songwriter I'm going to be. There was only one Hank Williams."

It was like a fire, and I rummaged around in my little bureau until I found a pencil and my notebook that I kept around, just in case. And I started writing, just like that.

>I know that I'm not great
>Some folks say I just imitate.
>Any more, I don't know
>I'm just doin' the best I can
>
>It's hard when you're standing in the shadow
>Of a very great man . . .

I laid down the pencil and looked at the first verse, and I knew it was going to be called "Standing in the Shadows," and I wanted to shout "Hey, that's me. That's my life!" I looked over and saw that my hand was shaking. Up front, I could hear Mother talking and the poker game going full tilt. I could feel the road rolling by under the big wheels. And on the paper in front of me, I could see my life. My hand was still shaking when I picked up the pencil again.

> You know as I travel around from town to town,
> I have a whole lot of Daddy's old fans and friends come around.
> And they say, "I know Hank would be so proud of you if he was still with us today.
> We're all so glad, and we know he would be too, that you're carrying on his great music this way . . .

> They tell me Hank Williams was the all-time great,
> And we know now you'll be just as good as your dad.
> But I just smile and say, "There'll never be another Hank Williams, folks,
> And that's what makes me and a whole lot of other people sad . . ."

A recitation—something to explain how I felt. How *I* felt, not how Daddy felt or anything else. A way to tell Daddy's fans who I was. Then the chorus again, and a second recitation:

> You see, there's so many times and nights
> I'm out there on that stage,
> And Lord, I feel things go through me
> And for just one minute it seems that
> I'm in another world.
> And that's when it always does something to me.

> The people they're all hollerin' and clappin' real loud,
> And while I'm out there just taking my bows,
> I look up toward the ceiling and say to myself:
> "Just listen, Daddy. Just listen to Bocephus and probably some of your old crowd."

> But as the show goes on, and the people clap and holler for more,
> And maybe I do another of those greatest of songs . . .
> That's the time that I know, although you're gone, your music will live on and on and on . . .

I was shaking even more when I finished, but I was so happy! It wasn't Daddy's and it wasn't Mother's and it wasn't handed to me on a platter. It was my song, and it was about my life, and even if it was a little maudlin here or there, I sure wasn't going to admit it! I looked down at my watch, and, miraculously, only twenty minutes had passed since I started writing. It seemed more like a lifetime.

I put the pencil away and tore off the sheet of paper. Then I worked as hard as I could to look, nonchalant as possible. When I thought I was composed enough, I took the paper up to the front of the bus.

"Mom," I said to Audrey. "I've, uh, been sort of working on a song, and I thought you . . . I mean, I'd sort of like for you to take a look at it."

Audrey smiled, and the front section of the bus lit up with that smile. "Sure," she said. "Let me see it."

I handed over the paper, and I was scared. I was even more scared when I saw the expression on her face start to change. First she was smiling; then the smile changed into a sort of half-frown, and I could see the wrinkles forming across her face. When she finished reading the song and started to hand me back the paper, I realized she was crying, and that everything had gotten very quiet in the bus.

"Oh, Hank," she said, tears rolling down her cheeks. "Oh, Hank, it's wonderful!"

I felt almost guilty, with the men on the bus trying hard not to stare at me, and my mother holding me and crying and all. I also felt proud, prouder of that song than of anything else I'd done.

When we got back to Nashville, we were in the studio within a few days, cutting "Standing in the Shadows."

It was a hit, and that made me feel really good. "Long Gone Lonesome Blues" had been a hit, but it was as much Daddy's hit as it was mine, and deep down inside I knew that, although I didn't like to admit it. My next two releases after the first one hadn't done too well at all—"Endless Sleep" hung around the bottom of the charts, and "Is It That Much Fun to Hurt Someone" never made the charts at all. I'd written "Is It That Much Fun to Hurt Someone," but it was nothing like "Standing in the Shadows." It's all the difference between night and day, between craftsmanship and

96

inspiration. This song had been given to me, and I felt almost privileged.

There was another surprise waiting for me in Nashville that year, and I can't really say that I felt all that privileged—although I felt guilty as hell for *not* feeling privileged.

Mother bought me a car.

Well, not just a car. I guess it started life as a Pontiac. Then Nudie, the incredible western tailor, fixed it up a little. Like adding 547 silver dollars here and there, fifteen silver horseshoes, twelve large pistols, three rifles, ten small pistols, seven silver horses, and seventeen silver horseheads. Not to mention a saddle between the driver and the passenger, air conditioning, and an automatic transmission.

"It's great publicity," Audrey said.

"I love it, Mother. It's really great," I said, dying inside. How could I drive that *thing*? What girl in her right mind would sit in a car covered with silver dollars and chrome-plated gun handles? "I love it."

"Well, just sit in it and have your picture taken. Drive it to a couple of shows, maybe drive it around town a little," she said. "It'll be worth it."

I hoped so. It cost $22,000. I'd have much rather taken a nice hunting trip or gone to a couple of Civil War battlefields. Now, that was what was interesting—just nosing around old battlefields and the like, reliving history in your mind.

"I love it."

So I drove it around town, as little as possible, and, sure enough, I saw my picture in the paper quite a bit. "Car a rolling mint," the captions said, and I always looked embarrassed. But two things happened to take my mind off cruising around Nashville, one professional and one very personal.

On the professional front, after much hemming and hawing and head-scratching, I'd been tapped to do the music for *Your Cheatin' Heart*, the film biography of my father, starring George Hamilton.

Personally, I'd discovered girls in a big way.

12

The Cheatin' Heart Special

Your Cheatin' Heart was a turning point in many ways and not all of them were good. I wasn't first choice to do the music for the movie—actually, George Hamilton wanted to sing himself.

The Hollywood people were willing to go along. After all, George Hamilton was a pretty big star at the time, and his singing, bad as it was, might kick off some kind of recording career for him, which would help the movie, which would help him, and on and on and on. Lucky for me that the person who wasn't all that interested in helping George Hamilton's singing career was Wesley Rose, of Acuff-Rose. Wesley and his father, Fred Rose, had worked with Daddy his whole professional life, and the relationship between Fred Rose and Hank Williams was a deep one. Wesley had been a friend for as long as I can remember, and he had advised Mother about my career. In the game of *Your Cheatin' Heart*, Wesley Rose held the trump card: Acuff-Rose was the sole licensing agent for Daddy's songs, and Wesley was the man who said whether those songs could be used at all. Without the songs, there wouldn't be much of a movie.

Wesley said he wanted me to sing the sound track, and that was that.

But who was better equipped to sing Daddy's songs than me? I wanted to do that soundtrack very badly. Daddy had been on my mind more and more lately, and I felt this nagging urge to do something to honor him, to show him, if that's the right word, that I still respected him above all other men. And what could be better than a film tribute, the story of Hank Williams in picture and song? I was determined to make this a masterpiece.

Your Cheatin' Heart might have been destined for a lot of things, but being a masterpiece wasn't one of them. This was *Hollywood*, and this was 1964, and it wasn't enough that Daddy suffered. He had to suffer more, bigger, and better! It wasn't enough that he drank. He had to drink *oceans*. For example, the producers almost insisted that, in the movie, Hank be drunk when he went on stage for the first time at the Opry. George Hamilton wanted Hank to be drunk at that performance. It would make a better story. It would also tarnish one of country music's sacred legends, throw a little dirt on those seven encores that first night at the Opry. In that particular case, Wesley Rose still held the big stick, and he used it, again and again.

Something was happening, though, with Mother. She was the adviser to *Your Cheatin' Heart*, and she was rewriting her part little by little. She suggested minor changes, and the producer, Sam Katzman, agreed. The changes taken by themselves didn't amount to much—instead of suggesting that Hank do this show or record that song, maybe she ordered him to do it—but, taken as a whole, there was a disturbing pattern emerging.

On screen, my mother was becoming a bitch, and she was totally blind to it.

It's important, she kept saying. We've got to say how it was. It was me, she told the producers, who pushed Hank into stardom. She made him go to Nashville. She found Fred and Wesley Rose and made them listen. Hank was a drunk and without ambition, and if it wasn't for Audrey there never would have been a Hank Williams. The movie *had* to reflect that. People *had* to know.

"It's a mistake, Audrey," Wesley Rose told her. "It's a bad mistake, and one you're going to be sorry for. Do you want to be a shrew? A harpy? Well, that's how you're going to look when this movie comes out. People aren't going to like what they see."

"Damn it, Wesley! Stop it! I know what I did, and that's all I'm trying to tell people. That's all!" Mother said. "I won't let you take Hank Williams away from me!"

"You're going to have to live with that movie, Audrey, and so is Bocephus. Think about him. How's he going to defend you with you up there on that screen?" Wesley was mad, and, as a rule, Wesley Rose didn't get mad.

"You're not going to take Hank Williams away from me." Period. No discussion. When the time came for Mother to sign the papers to renew the copyrights for Daddy's songs—something that had to be done before the movie could be completed—she insisted on having her lawyers go over the forms time and time again, and she refused to talk to Wesley about it. It was never spoken aloud, but no one, least of all Wesley Rose, doubted that Audrey was afraid Acuff-Rose was trying to cheat her out of her rightful money. When she finally signed the papers, it was grudging. Wesley Rose wasn't our friend anymore, and Mother was a changed woman.

Your Cheatin' Heart was one of the biggest money grossers of 1966, a surprise runaway hit, and the soundtrack album quickly sold over a million copies. Mother told the Nashville newspaper: "I feel sad and happy at the same time. George Hamilton plays Hank and Susan Oliver plays my part. But hearing Hank Junior on the soundtrack reminds me of his father. He sounds so much like his dad, and his mannerisms are the same . . ."

We wasted no time in getting on the road, in a refurbished bus now christened "The Cheatin' Heart Special." It was hard to imagine, but I was close to the top of the business. Hank Williams Junior and the Cheatin' Heart Special were the biggest draw in country music. From a novelty act to a superstar in one easy lesson—WHAM! BAM! It seemed so simple. It was all mine for the taking, and I reached out and took it.

And something changed. Some indefinable something shifted a few degrees, and the world was a slightly different place. There were new rules, and the old rules were fully revealed for the first time. Mother would never be a star in her own right. What she was—and I saw this for the first time—was the protector of the Legend of Hank Williams. That was her reason for being. She was enemies of anyone who would detract from that legend, and the absolute protector of the legend's friends. What I was was a son in search of a father. I saw it so clearly now! If I wanted to know Daddy, I had to search for him. If I wanted to be the son of Hank Williams, I was going to have to prove myself worthy; I was going to have to understand how Hank Williams felt, why he did the things he did. It was not enough to be simply a part—a big part, sure—of the legend. That was the same thing as being a bystander. I had to *live* the legend.

And that was a solitary quest. Mother couldn't help. That was the revelation.

"It's just wonderful, Hank. It's an opportunity that you just can't pass up," Mother said on the way to the studio. I believed her, because the "it" fit in perfect with my new feelings about Daddy. What we'd done was to take the recordings of my father's and strip off a good bit of the accompaniment. Then I would go in and sing harmony over my father's tracks. The result would be two albums, "duets" between myself and Daddy.

It really wasn't anything special in the way of a recording session, except that it was easier than most. I was just doing harmonies with a voice I knew better than my own, singing songs I must've sung in the cradle.

When they played the first tape back, someone in the control room made a face and said "Eerie," and I think he's lucky he

102

didn't have his head snapped off. When you think of it, though, it *was* eerie. It sounded sort of like an overdub, where one artist will go back and add his voice a second time to the recording, except that there was just enough difference in my voice and Daddy's to remind you that there were two different people singing. Some people said that listening to the record gave them the same feeling as when somebody walked across their grave—sort of a little hair-raising along the back of the neck.

No matter, because I was proud of it. It seemed I was pretty proud of almost anything I did that had to do directly with Daddy, and that's the direction Mother was pushing me in. (I remember once that Johnny Cash, who never snaps at anyone, almost snapped at Mother. "Loosen up a little, Audrey," he told Mother. "Let him be Hank Williams Junior for a while.") But the records did well, especially with Daddy's older fans.

There was some rumblings, though. For the first time there was the slight hint of a backlash—nothing big, nothing I would even take much notice of until years later. But for the first time some people shook their heads disapprovingly (out of my sight, of course), and for the first time I got some genuinely bad reviews. Enough, they said, is enough. What are they going to do next, the reviews asked, take the coffin on tour? No one ever showed me those reviews, although I wish someone had. But I was fifteen years old, and I probably wouldn't have read them anyway.

13

The Cheatin' Heart Special—II

She must have had a name, but nobody bothered to tell it to me. All I knew was that I'd been drooling since she walked backstage at Cobo Hall, where I was getting ready to become a star. Mostly, she wasn't paying any attention to me. She moved through the backstage area with practiced grace, carrying on many small conversations with the band members, the performers, and the various local dignitaries that always seem to gather backstage at any big concert.

She was almost as tall as me, and I was a big fourteen-year-old—six feet tall and over 150 pounds. She was dressed in black, and she had red hair. I don't know which were higher, her heels or her breasts. Someone backstage told me she was a journalist, here special to cover the concert. And I had fantasies—Lord, did I ever have fantasies! She was older— twenty-eight, someone said—but I would dominate her. I'd show her. Fourteen-year-olds think things like that.

She was in the back of my mind when I went on stage, and when I came off, all flushed with my victory, one of the band members finally managed to drag me away from my admirers.

"Hank, listen here," he said urgently in an exaggerated stage whisper. "Listen, you know that redheaded piece of ass you've been mooning over ever since you got here?"

I shook my head yes, wondering what was going on.

"You want her?"

I must have looked like I'd just seen my first *Playboy* Magazine.

"What?" I asked, genuinely befuddled. "What do you mean?"

"Want her, stupid," he said, leering. "Want her. Do you want to fuck her or what? She's really got the hots for you, you know."

"Fuck her?" I could feel my blood rush to my head. I could feel my palms starting to sweat. I was shaking a little, and the bulge in my pants must have been noticeable for miles and miles. "Fuck her? Shit yes!" Boy oh boy—the real thing! No ninth-grade back seat bangs with *coitus interruptus* for me!

"I'll be back in a minute." And he was gone, leaving me wondering if somebody was getting ready to play one hell of a joke on old Bocephus. Boy, I hoped not, touching the bulge for just a second. I hoped not!

"Hank, there's somebody here I'd like you to meet," the band member said as he returned with her in tow. She was even more beautiful than I remembered! Her breasts were big, but not too big. Her legs belonged in a museum somewhere. I was pretty close to speechless.

"Hello," I said cleverly. I was lucky to get that out.

"I believe we've met already," she said, and her voice almost made me lose control completely. Like warm honey being poured all over me. To hell with stardom.

We went to one of the little rooms backstage. There are always lots of those rooms at every big concert hall—enough dressing rooms and cubbyholes to dress an army. The people who design auditoriums are no fools.

We went into the room—there was a couch and a mirror and a dresser with light bulbs all around it—and locked the door behind us.

"I liked your show, Hank," she said, and I thanked her. I was sweating all over and I hoped she didn't notice! My hands were shaking, and I knew she'd see it and laugh. "Damn," I thought. "This is a lot tougher than the performance!"

"I don't do this with just everyone, you know."

"Oh no!" I blurted. "I know that. I mean, I know you're not that kind of girl!"

She smiled, and then she kissed me for a long time, her tongue exploring for what seemed like hours. She was still smiling when she broke off the kiss, stepped back, and reached around to unzip her dress. I think my tongue was hanging out, and I prayed I wasn't doing anything totally gross like panting or drooling or something. She let the black dress slide to the floor, then she stepped out of it. She was wearing a white bra, white bikini panties, and a white garterbelt holding up her dark stockings. She unhooked the bra in the front and let her full breasts bounce free. Her nipples were dark brown and hard, and I was hotter than a fox in a forest fire!

"Gol-leee!" I whispered. She heard me and laughed, just a little and not threatening at all. Then she stepped forward and unzipped my pants, unhooked my hand-tooled leather belt, and cupped my oh-so throbbing penis in her hand. Her tongue reached out to caress it, and I put my hands on her red hair. It was just like the boys in the band described it to me on those long drives back to Nashville! It was goooood!

Then I thought of Sharon, my high school girlfriend. Sharon had almost cried when I'd touched her breast a couple of months ago. But she'd let me. She'd even let me put my hand under her sweater for just a second, and I'd pinched her nipple and felt it harden under my hand. Once she'd touched my zipper and rubbed for just a second.

"Oh, Hank, I love you. You know I do." she'd said. "But I've got to know if you love me, too. I just can't let you go all the way. Oh, Hank!"

"I love you, Sharon," I'd told her. "I love you more than anything."

And she still wouldn't let me do more than touch!

Boy, things were different now! Sharon was a long way away.

My new friend raised up and kissed me on the lips, and she was still kissing me while she undressed me. Then she slipped out of her panties and stockings—she was a redhead *everywhere*—and straddled me while I lay back on the couch. She pumped and moaned and I guess I shook like a little billy goat. "Oh, oh Hank . . ." she moaned. "You're not at all like a fourteen-year-old kid! Not at all!" I grunted, and I came too soon, and she didn't seem to mind at all. I didn't either, 'cause now I was a *real* man.

We spent a lot of time that evening in that little room while the greats of the Grand Ole Opry were on stage, and it was beyond description. At least, it was for me. For six years I'd been on the road, and on every one of those trips I'd heard about this from the guys in the band, from the other performers, from almost everyone except Mother. When you went on the road, they said, there are a few compensations for what you have to give up. The bottle was one of them. The pills were another. But nothing, son, nothing at all beats the women! Your daddy knew that, and you'll learn it too.

I had learned, brother, had I learned!

She kissed me one more time, then she got up and got dressed. She smiled and waved on the way out, and I never saw her again, and I don't know her name.

I just lay back on the couch, feeling sweaty and sore and good all over. I couldn't wait to get back to Sharon. Boy, would I have a few things to show her!

After that I was never alone unless I particularly wanted to be. A lot of country singers act real pious and say—at least, for publication—that they've never even met a "groupie" on the road. Snuff queens. I've seen country singers so sincere that I almost believed them, and I knew they were lying. Because there were always women, as many as you could want in as many different varieties as you could think of. Some were pretty, some downright ugly, all willing. At first, when you're young, you wonder what makes them do it, spend some time with a man who doesn't even know their name and cares even less. I've slept with some very intelligent women, college graduates who want nothing more than twenty minutes of my time. Women with families, with husbands who love them, who just want to drop by the room for a few minutes and perform an unnatural act. Sometimes their husbands knew and approved.

After a while, though, you don't think about it much, any more than you'd think about water coming out of a tap when you turned it on. They were just there, and they were there for your convenience.

"Hey Hank, drop what you're doing and come up here to room 504, we've got a couple of hot pieces and we need a little help . . ."

"Which'd you rather have, the blonde with zits or the chubby redhead . . ."

"I'd better get back to the room or Mother's going to come in and I'll be in trouble! Trouble!"

"This one wants to meet you, Hank. Just as soon as I get finished with her. I think she wants us all . . ."

Or the time my friend and fellow performer, who shall remain nameless in deference to his wife of many years, who was having such a good time with this one little queen that he ended up, ahem, spending himself in her shoe. That was about the funniest thing I'd ever seen—so funny that I couldn't pay attention to what *I* was doing (we were in adjoining beds). To this day, he still asks girls their shoe size when he first meets them.

Or the night we locked Johnny Cash out and wouldn't let him in, and all night long he just stood at one door or another moaning real soft, "Hank, come on, son, let me in. What's going on in there? Let me in, please . . ."

Yes, I know what it sounds like, but I'll make no apologies for my behavior. Nor will I lie about it to make me sound better or more pious or whatever. The road is its own world, with its own moralities and its own laws. Nothing from the outside counts even a little bit. In the country song, there's always a distinction between a honky-tonk angel and the girl who waits at home. On the road, that distinction is very real.

14

I'd Rather Be Gone

"You're just going to have to understand how badly you've been hurt," the doctor is saying. Eight days have passed, and I'm still alive. So alive that I want to go home. "You're looking at another six weeks in here, and that's a good estimate. Given the kind of surgery you've gone through, six weeks is lucky."

I shake my head agreeably. Actually, I'm still very content. It's an odd sort of contentment, one that has its roots, I think, in resignation. And I am resigned, to the life of a hermit that fate has chosen for me. I have been dealt the cards, and now I'm learning how to play with them. It's a pretty good feeling.

I work on my music, and it's improving by leaps and bounds. Maybe there's something to the other senses compensating, because with my vision, hearing, smell, taste all impaired, my sense of touch is superb. My feel of the strings was never better, I never hit a string awkwardly to make it buzz. The music grows more fluid every day, and the nurses and orderlies are starting to look forward to my concerts. Even the doctors are optimistic—they want me to rehabilitate myself.

But I feel something gnawing at my sense of security. Guns are a large part of my life, just as they were a large part of Daddy's. The woods and the hunt mean a lot to me, and I am—was, rather—a fine shot, a skill built up over the years. But it's a skill that's totally dependent on the coordination of my right hand and my right eye. Which is all well and good, except that my right eye may never work again.

To some people that might seem a small matter—so he never shoots again. He's alive, isn't he? But those people can't understand how much a part of my life guns and the outdoors had become. They can't appreciate the mechanical perfection in a fine piece of machinery like a Weatherby rifle or an old Smith and Wesson revolver. They can't appreciate the constant competition between a man and himself as he tries to make the group of shots on the target smaller and smaller. I've always loved sports, but for my money there's nothing to compare with the thrill that comes to a good marksman, be he a hunter or a target shooter, because the success or failure depends solely on that man. There are no other excuses. Or maybe that person can't appreciate the hunt, that oldest of man's sports. Maybe he'd prefer to do his killing more cleanly, at $4.00 per pound, cellophane wrapped, at his local supermarket. When I have steak, I'd rather know how it came to my table and dispense with the illusions.

But I am afraid, and that fear is growing. I finally ask Dick to bring me a revolver, with its cylinder removed so the nurses won't panic. Besides, Montana is a state chock full of outdoorsmen and outdoorswomen. Even in the hospital nobody's going to get hysterical over the presence of a handgun. This isn't New York City, thank heavens!

Dick brings me the gun, and I set about the arduous task of training myself to shoot with my *left* eye instead of my right. That's tough, just about as tough as learning to write with your left hand instead of your right. But every day I practice, sighting out the window of the hospital toward the mountains. Sometimes I pretend we're on a hunt, and I'm sighting down a buffalo or an elk. Some-

112

times I remember hunts I've been on, and I relive them and work with the revolver.

Each day it gets a little easier. Every day the odd pattern of twisting my head around to line up my left eye with my right hand seems more and more natural. The doctors are very happy, because I'm training myself to fight whatever handicaps I can, and work around those I can't. They say it's a good sign.

The rest of my day is usually taken up with the mail, and that's about the third thing that really keeps me going. We get tons of mail a day, from friends and fans and just plain well-wishers. I read every one of those letters, and they mean a lot. I've even got mail from everybody from the Marshall Tucker Band to Ernest Tubb, and that's just about as far from A to Z as you're likely to get!

I wish my well-meaning relatives would get lost, especially my not-so-well-meaning wife. All she cares about is the rodeo, and she's badgering everybody within sight to tell her where the nearest rodeo is so she and her friend Sherry can drive over to see it. Rodeos are not high on my list of priorities, but I don't say anything. I decide to say as little as possible to Gwen, in the hopes that she'll read my mind and go away.

Dick Willey and friends are holding the line against the worst of the jackals, although Dick keeps saying when he thinks that I can't hear him that "It's worse than a three-ring circus!" Mother is in bad shape, but she's holding up better than I expected—I never claimed that she was anything but tough. Cash and Kilgore still provide on-and-off comedy relief, and it's still appreciated. But I'm chafing a little.

Damn it, I want to go home!

Later in the day—it's the fifteenth day since the fall—the door opens and a parade of doctors walk into the room. They line up in a horseshoe around the bed, and for a minute my gut contracts in a little knot. Jesus! Maybe they're going to tell me I died yesterday!

"I'll be damned if we understand it," says Dr. Dewey, "But there's nothing more we can do for you here. You might as well go home."

The other doctors nod in agreement.

"You might as well go," he says again, as if he himself can't believe it. "Everything's just healing up great. You're easy to work with. You're not allergic to any drugs. As we see it, your recovery is at such a point that there's nothing to be gained by you staying in the hospital. Go home, Hank."

I could kiss them all, right then and there!

That afternoon they finish clipping out the stitches, instruct Betty Willey what to do with me once she gets me home, and, after the appropriate goodbyes and well-wishes, I'm on my way home.

Well, not exactly home. Where I'm going is Dick and Betty's main home in Polson, Montana, on the shore of Flathead Lake at the southernmost tip of Glacier National Park. It's some of the most beautiful country in America, and it seems to be the ideal place for a fellow looking to do a little recuperation.

Polson is about ninety miles from Missoula, and old Dick is doing the driving. I know it's a beautiful drive, 'cause I've made it many, many times on my own, but I'm not seeing too much today. I look like something else, maybe a junkie or someone equally unsavory. I've got on shades to protect my eyes, and a stocking cap to cover the round hole that's still the main feature of my forehead. I'm so thin I look like a ghost. My vision's not too good—especially in my right eye—and any loud noise is downright painful.

As we drive along, Dick points out buffalo and elk in the preserves, and all I see are blurs. When we get to the house in Polson, I'm too tired to even take in the view. I go straight to bed. Gwen is here, and I suggest, not without a touch of malice, that maybe she'd like to spend the night in the bedroom with me.

"I don't think you're up to it yet, Hank," she says, and spends the night in the adjoining room. The next day, with a lot of bleating and moaning on her part and stony silence on mine, she goes back to Nashville. There are newspaper reports later that quote her as being very worried about my health, and that any talk of a divorce is just that—talk. That's pretty funny, I think.

* * *

114

It's September, and there's winter definitely in the air. Sometimes I sit outside in the chill and stare into the wilderness, and my mind floats back up to that mountain. Sometimes I relive every minute, step by step. I feel myself falling, know that I'm dying. I spend hours on the side of the mountain, drifting between death and life and finally choosing the latter. I know I'm a different person now, and the task seems to be integrating the new person into the old life. I decide, though, what I will *not* do. I will not testify. I will not come down off the mountain and explain how I've found Jesus, although it's clear that I could make a quick and easy fortune doing just that. I won't say that I wasn't tempted, just for a second—a quick trip to a recording studio and one gospel record and whammo—superstardom again.

But no, that wasn't the lesson of the mountain. I spend a lot of time thinking of that lesson, which is so simple I can't imagine having not learned it a long time ago—if you're going to live, live. Just live your life to the best of your abilities, and if you need strength, it's there for the asking. A simple prayer will suffice.

When I feel a little stronger, we go down to Missoula to buy me a better guitar for my practice. We find an old Martin D-18 at one of the music stores in town, and I can't wait to get it back to Polson. When we do get it back, it's every bit as good as I had hoped. The tone is mellow, full, and rich. It speaks of a craftsmanship beyond my ability to play it, and I'm determined to master that guitar. I grow to love the way my fingers feel when they move across those strings, the tingly sensation that travels up my fingers and sends shivers down my spine. Before the fall, I always fancied myself a pretty fair guitar player. I know now that I was nothing more than a rank amateur compared to what I could be. I practice a lot.

As soon as I'm able, Dick starts me playing Ping-Pong, and damnation, that's hard! The little ball seems possessed by a mean-spirited little demon who delights in whizzing past my paddle. It's frustrating as hell, but each day I seem a little better. My eyes, such as they are, have reintroduced themselves to my hands, and the two are making an effort at mutual cooperation. It'll be a long time before I ever bring Willey to his knees with a paddle, but I've no doubts that the day will eventually come.

I hike around the house, trying to take longer and longer walks each day. I am pushing hard. I *have* to push that hard, because there's a lot I have to do. I have a sense of my own mortality now. Beautiful as Polson is, there are still roads I have to travel. My album is back there in Nashville, and they're rushing to release it. If I could tour . . .

The doctors, of course, say that's out of the question. I've proven them wrong before, and I'm going to prove them wrong again.

I hike and I play Ping-Pong and I throw the football to Walt, who seems to look on me as something of an older brother. His own ordeal on the mountain doesn't seem to have left any obvious scars, but Betty says sometimes he cries out in his sleep, incoherent screams about someone dying.

I miss food. Boy, do I miss food! My jaws are still wired together, and I think if I have another liquid anything, I'm going to scream. Betty, God bless her, is doing the best she can, which is pretty darn good. She's a health nut, and she makes me special milk shakes with every single vitamin and mineral and nutrient in the whole world in them, and, boy, I'll bet they're great for me.

If they only weren't green—pale green. If they only didn't taste like mulched cardboard and cottage cheese. Dick calls them "puke shakes," and I drink every last drop. Mmmmmmm, good. Boy, I wish I could pucker my lips! I have this vision knocking around my head, and it's a vision of tuna fish: A huge, gigantic tuna fish salad on white bread, with lots of mayo on the side. That sandwich is just about as beautiful as any woman I've ever seen. It's the sort of sandwich a Rembrandt or Da Vinci would like to render into immortality so everyone could see it just as I do. Sometimes at night I'd dream about that sandwich and wake up in the morning drooling. "Just you wait," I think, somewhat grimly. "Just you wait, sandwich. I'm gunning for you."

My afternoons center around Yosemite Sam, oddly enough. Every afternoon at four thirty cartoons come on television, and the main cartoon is "Yosemite Sam." I look forward to that almost as much as I look forward to my tuna fish sandwich. "I'll get you, you varmiiite!" old Yosemite yells, then he just blasts away! I spend a lot of time shouting, "I'll get you, you varmiiite!" It feels good, and I like it.

When there's nothing left to do, I study. Mostly I study the history of western Montana until I know every battle, every Indian, by name. That kind of information will be good to know if I have to make my life here in Montana as a hermit. I want to cover all the bases.

I'm studying one afternoon when Dick comes in.

"I've got to go down to the Big Hole to load up some cattle," Dick says. "Think you'd like to take a ride down there?"

I jump at the chance. It's a long drive, four or five hours, and I'm pretty tired when we finally get there. But there's the cabin, just the way I remember it. It seems like only yesterday when I was here last, so happy to be back in the mountains. The cows are still milling around outside like they owned the place. There's more snow than I remember on top of the mountains. The gun cases are still there, still open and ready to go. Dick builds a fire in the fireplace, and after we warm up a little, Dick picks up a .45 Colt revolver that I'd given him a few years back and suggests we go outside to do a little target shooting.

I am all knotted up inside. I am scared. But I rummage around and find my own .45 and a few shells. We go outside and set up the target.

"Let me see what I can do with this thing," Dick says. He eyes the target, about twenty-five yards down the way, cocks the Colt, and lets fly. The shot goes wild, barely catching a corner of the target. I can't stand it any longer.

"Give me that thing," I say, and take the Colt. Just like in the hospital, I cock my head so my left eye lines up with the sights. The gun feels steady in my hand as I cock it, then *squeeeeze* the trigger. The .45 roars, and as I lower the gun I see Dick beaming like a new daddy. There's a new hole in the target, dead center in the bull's-eye.

"Not *too* shabby for a one-eyed hunter who just fell off a mountain," Dick says. "Not too bad."

I get out my own Colt and fire three quick shots. All three are in the X-ring, dead center. I can still shoot!

Dick slaps me gently on the back, and I feel wonderful. That's one more step in the direction I want to go.

Then it's time to go back to Missoula to get my jaws unwired, and I can hardly wait. Food! Real food! The thought is almost too much to bear.

My jaws are pretty well wired together, and Dr. Murray, the plastic surgeon, is grinning about it.

"You'd better hold on to something, 'cause this wire is coming from behind your eyeball," he says. Although he's smiling, I know he's serious. I grab the side of the chair as the doctor clips the various other wires in my jaw. Then he takes a pair of pliers, grips the end of the wire, and *pulls*.

There's an awful grating noise, exactly like fingers scraping across a blackboard, except it's wire scraping across my jaw. Lots of wire. Blood is spurting all over the place, and Willey, who's decided to stay in the room with me, has turned very, very pale.

"Holy Christ!" he says. "That hurts! Jesus, that hurts!"

With a *thwummp!* the first wire pops out of my head, and Dr. Murray grabs the second. *Grate, thwummp!* And in a rain of blood I can suddenly move my jaws again. Not much. Not after two months with them wired together. But there's a little movement, and it feels great. Let me at those steaks, boy! Just point me toward a kitchen!

And that's all I can think about on the way back to Polson. I conjure up mountains of food, gulping it all down after tearing it to pieces with my new, improved jaws. The ninety miles pass fast, and as soon as I'm out of the car, I'm headed toward Betty's kitch-

118

en. I find a can of tuna fish, pull the mayonnaise out of the refriger-
ator, and go to work in earnest. The finished creation is magnificent. A work of art. The ultimate tuna fish sandwich. I almost hate
to eat it. Almost.

I sit down at the table with Dick and Betty and Walt and Chris,
their daughter, and let the awesome sandwich speak for itself.
Then I lift it up, slowly, to savor the maximum effect. I open my
mouth as wide as it will go, insert the sandwich, and bite down with
all my might.

Only nothing happens.

I really chomp down then. Then I take the sandwich out of my
mouth. There's not even teeth marks in the bread.

Damn it! No teeth! No muscles!

I throw the sandwich onto my plate, and it bounces. I'm beside
myself with frustration, and Dick and Betty are almost hysterical
with laughter. When we all calm down, Betty cuts the magnificent
sandwich into tiny pieces, and I have the last laugh.

Now bring on those steaks!

The days pass quickly, and they're busy, full days. My plans for
my own recovery are going well, and it seems like there's nothing I
can't conquer with a little work. Except for one tiny problem.
There's this woman who keeps calling me, and her name is Becky.
I met her just before the fall, and she can't quite understand that
I'm never going to be able to be around women again. I wish I
could make her understand, because, frankly, I like her a lot and I
don't want to see her hurt. If she ever sees me, there's no way she
couldn't be hurt. No sirree, there's never going to be any more
women in my life, and she's going to have to accept that the same
way I did.

She's tough. She'll live. I've got to make her understand that.

15

Superstar Blues

I was bored as only a seventeen-year-old can be bored, sitting in that motel room in Augusta, Georgia, killing time before the night's show. I'd tried reading a little, but I'd been on the road too long and couldn't bring myself to concentrate on a page of print. The only thing on television was some soap opera, "General Misery" or something, and after ten deadeningly slow minutes of that, I shut off the set in disgust and flopped down on the bed.

Darn! I'd been to more exciting wakes!

As if on cue, the telephone rang.

"Is this Hank Williams Junior?" the exceedingly female voice on the other end said.

"Ah ha, a diversion," I thought.—"It sure is."

"Well, you don't know me, but my name is Gwen. Gwen Yeargain. And I'm calling from Missouri," she said. My plans for the afternoon collapsed. "What I'm calling about—well, I'm actually embarrassed to tell you—I mean, I have this bet with my mother that I can find out where you are and call you. And I just won the bet!"

"A bet?" Great, just great.

"And now that I've talked to you, I think I'd like to meet you. I'd like to meet you very much."

"Well, uh, I'm in Augusta today. Maybe if you told me a little more about yourself. . . ." Sure, I'd had some wild times, but I was still part shy kid. Especially when I was being hustled over the telephone.

"Of course! Well, I'm nineteen-years old and I'm a model and an actress. I mean, I've got a part in a local play, and they say I'm pretty good. My figure is 36–24–37, I've got long black hair, and some people have even said I was beautiful. So you think you might like to meet me?"

A model! Little alarm bells were going off inside my head and below my belt. "From here I go to Little Rock on Friday night . . ."

"Fine," she said. "I'll be there. Remember, my name is Gwen, and don't worry about finding me. I'll find you."

Now *that* was a good way to break up a dull afternoon, I thought as I hung up. It was almost like waiting for Christmas, getting through the show in Augusta and heading for Little Rock. I was so excited I could barely talk about it.

By the time of the show, I was in a real fair-thee-well, and I went out there on stage and just tore 'em up. I was playing to a special audience of one.

She came backstage after the show, a vision. Compared to her, my imagination looked like a pauper. She was everything she said she was, and a darn sight more.

"Golllleeeee," I whispered to no one in particular.

"Hank? Hello, I'm Gwen Yeargain."

And I'm in love. "Pleased to meet you,"

"Pretty clever," I thought. I sure wish I had a rock to kick so I could stand there and go, "Aw, shucks, ma'am." Sometimes I wished I was older than I was.

"Let's go somewhere we can talk, okay?"

Had she suggested it, I would have walked off the end of a bridge. Instead, we went out for coffee, and we talked. And talked,

122

and talked. I don't even remember about what. Whatever two people talk about when they're trying not to talk about what's on both their minds. Hours passed very fast, and pretty soon she had to go back to Missouri.

"Uh, listen," I said. "Me and Cash are going to Chattanooga for a few days to crawl around in caves and look for minié balls and Civil War stuff"—Cash and I did that a lot. I was always afraid I'd lose him in one of those caves and never see him again. He was always crawling off somewhere where he shouldn't—"and I could get you a ticket if you'd like to meet me there. Then we'd have a few days together and . . ."

I let the implication hang, mainly because I was too young and too scared to articulate it.

"That sounds really good," Gwen says. "I'll meet you in Chattanooga, then."

Then she was gone, and I was somewhere on Cloud Nine. Nineteen! She was an older woman, and she was beautiful. A model and an actress! She wasn't at all like Sharon, my at-home girlfriend, who'd been my girlfriend for years and years. And she wasn't at all like the women on the road, nameless faces and bodies that just passed through for the evening. I think that's what attracted me most of all. My experience with women was strangely limited. My experience with strong women was my mother. I'd started making a distinction between home-women and road-women. Home-women were patient and loving; they were good, and they stayed in the background. Road-women, on the other hand, were willing and available. The only thing they had in common with the women at home was that they too didn't ask anything from me. No real commitments. But Gwen tipped me off that there might be a third kind, one that I was absolutely unacquainted with—self-assured, poised, and knowing her own mind.

I couldn't wait to get to Chattanooga!

And when it happened, it was better than I ever could have imagined. We spent three days in Chattanooga, just Gwen and I, and then I took her to the Opry on Saturday night. Then I told her I wanted to get engaged to her. She laughed and said she loved me, too. We talked about it a lot, there in our cabin, then she had to go back to Missouri. "I've got a job, you know," she said. "I can't spend all my time just running around with you."

In equal parts, I wanted to marry her and I never wanted to see her again. She was too much like the road-women to totally give myself to; too much of something else again to totally dismiss. After I came down off the cloud, I decided I never wanted to see her again. With Sharon looking on, I called Gwen and told her just that. But Gwen Yeargain haunted my mind and my heart for a long time after that call.

Maybe it was naive of me to think that I could make a woman like Gwen disappear on a whim. I think I had a lot left to learn about women.

The play bill read, "Johnny Cash and Hank Williams Junior, in Concert," and I thought, "Well, here I am back in Detroit City again. Back at Cobo Hall, my first taste of stardom." I was fourteen then, nineteen now, and instead of a big Opry package show, it was just me and Cash. No opening act, no la-dee-dah paraphernalia. Me and Cash, the two biggest acts in country music, and we were going to go out there and knock 'em dead.

Which wouldn't be too hard, I thought. Johnny Cash and I had been touring a lot, and I'd really enjoyed it. Mother approved of Cash, and if she was going to have to cut me loose from her apron strings—which I was seeing to it that she was doing—it might as well be to someone like Cash.

Mother had changed a lot since *Your Cheatin' Heart*. She was more convinced than ever that Acuff-Rose was trying to twist her away from Daddy's royalties, and Wesley Rose had long since ceased to be a friend of the family, although he still produced some of Mother's efforts at recording. She saw me slipping away from her as well, and I think there were seeds of panic growing. What mollified her, though, was that I still accepted almost totally her teachings about Daddy, and in that sense I was still her creation.

Daddy's songs were still the backbone of my show, and it wasn't unusual for me to do a whole show of nothing but Daddy's songs, with maybe "Standing in the Shadows" and just a couple of my other numbers thrown in. The Hank Williams myth was still alive and flourishing, and I was still its chief priest. My search for my father still simmered, although I had temporarily pushed it aside for my adolescent pursuits.

I think that's one of the things that attracted me so much to Cash. He was a lot like I imagined Daddy must have been. We'd done some crazy things, Cash and I, and I was fascinated with his total disregard for his own safety and well-being. Like in the caves. If there was a sign that said, "Proceed No Further—Danger!", that was like waving a red flag in front of a bull. It darn near guaranteed that Cash would pick up his flashlight, get down on his belly if necessary, and crawl back into that hole. Oh, we always had some perfectly good reason. Both of us were Civil War nuts, and we were constantly looking for minié balls, bullets, rusted guns, and other relics to add to our collection. We'd heard once that there was a hidden Confederate ammo dump in the caves around Chattanooga, and that was all the excuse we ever needed to risk our lives in those dark holes.

Cash was a hard-living man in those days, just like I imagined Daddy must have been. There were pills and there was liquor, and there were shows where Cash almost couldn't make it and shows where he didn't show up at all. But when he hit that stage, it was like some automatic pilot demon took over, and he got out there and gave those people a show they'd remember. I admired that, and I grew very close to John Cash.

Because we were advancing the myth, Mother approved. It didn't take a particularly imaginative writer to look up there on stage and see Hank Williams Junior and the reincarnation of his Daddy, John R. Cash. I think we all realized that, and while we never went out and erected billboards that said it, we never went out of our way to deny it, either.

So Cash and I came to Cobo Hall fresh from a series of successes on stage, burned cars, destroyed hotel rooms, and stories that we've both done our best to forget.

We knew this show was going to be something special, but we had no idea how special until the people started filing in. There were two shows, an afternoon and an evening. We sold it out, both times. It was packed to the gills. When they totaled up the gate, it came to almost $100,000, which made it the largest money-grossing show in the history of country music.

We were great—a tour de force of country music. Cash and I were perfectly matched. He had the reputation of being country's finest recording star, and I was supposed to be its best showman. And boy, I worked at it! I'd been working with other instruments, especially the banjo, and I'd started working them into my act. I'd also been expanding my repertoire, adding a couple of bluegrass numbers (to highlight the banjo) and even a couple from George Jones, as well as my own stuff. I had, if I did say so myself, a pretty dynamic stage show, one more akin to rock and roll than most country shows, where somebody just walks out on stage and sings. I also had Nudie, the western tailor, make me a pink western suit with sequins—good taste is timeless.

I knew when I went on stage that this show was very different from my first Cobo Hall show. The audience was different, and they were expecting more from me. They had launched my career here, and if they thought I was trying to rip Daddy off, I think they were fully prepared to end my career just as soundly.

I went out there like a house a fire, singing my songs, singing Daddy's songs, moving around that stage like a demon. I worked—I sweated. I played the banjo and the piano, I sang George Jones' cryin'-in-your-beer ballads. I stood there in my pink Nudie suit and sang rock and roll to 'em, and, by God, they loved it! The loved me!

I got ovation after ovation after ovation, and Cash came out right behind me and laid them down again. It was a great moment for both of us, and the next day the reviews bordered on ecstatic. They called it one of the greatest shows in the history of country music.

126

"Cash got the audience with his great records, and Hank Jr. with his incredible virtuosity."

The show sent a shock wave straight back to Nashville, where the figure of $100,000 for a single concert was absolutely unheard of. That's why country music came in package shows—individual performers just didn't have that kind of pull. Cash and I did. That put us at the top of the top.

I'd like to say it had been a long, hard climb, from humble beginnings singing to cornstalks and broomsticks. Of course I'd be lying. It took me eleven years from the time of my first stage performance to become one of the top stars in country music, and I'd be lying if I didn't say I took a lot of it for granted. I worked hard. And I'd be lying to you if I didn't admit that I was good, damn good, in fact. But I had had a sort of rocket-assisted beginning. One might say I was powered by Hank Williams.

There was one thing about Cobo Hall the Second that reminded me about Cobo Hall the First, though. I'd been doing some duets with Penny Dehaven, a pretty well-known artist in her own right, and she was up there in Detroit with me. Aside from the fact that I had finally up and married someone else, Penny and I were *very* close friends, and she was amazed at how long I could go on performing after two full shows. I told her it was because I was a consummate professional, and everyone knew the show must go on.

Penny was no slouch herself. We had opened a chain of barbeque joints awhile back, Hank Williams Junior Barbeques, for an investment. This was the era of Minnie Pearl's Fried Chicken and all those fast-food celebrity tax write-offs, and I was supposed to make an appearance for the grand opening of my first joint. What I really wanted to do was spend the afternoon with Penny engaged in not as lucrative, but lots more interesting, activity. But I couldn't dodge the opening—especially since my new bride, Sharon, was going to be there—so I had an idea. Why don't we, I suggested, just take the tour bus to the opening. Somebody can drive us over, and we can retire to the back of the bus. What a great idea!

When I swaggered off that bus at the grand opening of Hank Williams Junior Barbeque, a more affable country singer you'd be hard pressed to find!

Ah, women. The perils of stardom. I purposely avoided getting involved with any other artists—Penny excepted—mostly because between the girl at home and the girls on the road I had my hands full. Also, I was never sure where other women artists fitted into my Scheme of Things. One woman artist, still one of the very biggest artists in country music, called me one night after a package show.

"Hank, I think you dropped your cufflink up here. Would you like to come up and get it?"

Boy, would I! She was such a big star, and I was such a kid. I beat a path up the elevator, knocked on the door to her room, and found her waiting, lying on top of her bed.

"Come on in, Hank."

She was wearing the thinnest of nightgowns, and her husband was reported to be insanely jealous. I gulped and went in.

"Here's your cufflink. Wanna drink?"

I shook my head yes and poured myself a shot of vodka from a bottle sitting open by the bed. Then I took a good, long look. I'd never seen her without her makeup on, and, bless us all, she was *old*! She was worn down. There were lots of wrinkles, and I thought that maybe this wasn't such a hot idea after all. I picked up my cufflink off the little table by the bed.

"Well, thanks for the drink, but I've got to be going," I said, heading for the door. She looked puzzled.

"Are you sure you don't want to stay for another drink or something?" she said.

"Uh, no, ma'am," I said. "Thanks again," as the door closed. "Close," I thought, leaning against the door. From now on I'm sticking to the girl back home and the girls on the road! That's all I can handle!

Nashville was changing, right underneath my superstardom. It was a change I wouldn't feel until later, but when it hit, nothing

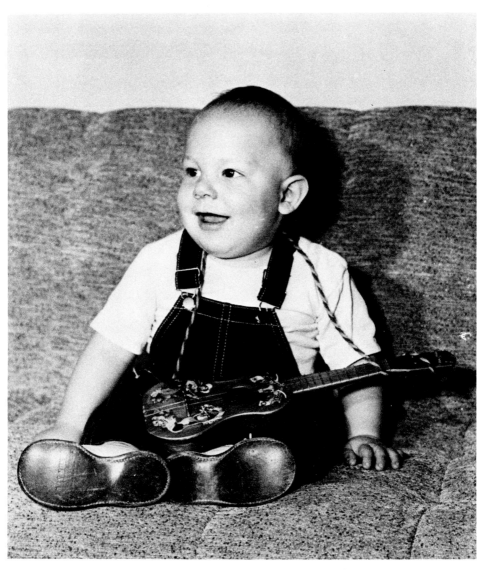

Here I am at the tender age of fourteen months, and would you believe I already know all the chords to my ukulele?

Our family tradition: my mother Audrey, sister Lycrecia, me (approximate age—eighteen months) and Daddy, decked out in his C&W finery. I'm surprised they didn't find a guitar for me to hold. (Henry Schofield)

A very little cowboy, here with my sister Lycrecia. For a while, she was going to be the singing star. Then she got smart. (Fabry Nashville)

And here's a snaggle-toothed grim from your basic six-year-old wonder kid. You'll notice the publicity pictures started early.

The big A's stood for Miss Audrey, my mother, of course, and this was from one of my earliest shows, which would make me around eight years old. Can you imagine people paying money to see *anybody* who looked like I did?

By this time I was getting pretty serious—I'm holding that guitar like I know what to do with it. And by the time this picture was taken, I did. I'd say I was around ten years old, and already an accomplished performer.

You can imagine the fan mail that this picture generated.
(Courtesy of MGM Records)

Sixteen years old and as tough as they come, that was me. I'd just played a rodeo in heaven knows where, and my friend here was the rodeo queen. Note the slicked back hair. (Jimmy Everett)

And here is the wonderful Hank Williams, Junior, showcar, flanked by hordes of admiring fans. This bastion of good taste is spending its reclining years in a museum in Pigeon Forge, Tennessee. By the way, be sure to notice my gold lame Nudie suit. (Clarence H. Lane.)

Politics and performers are touchy subjects—one should probably stay clear of the other, to tell the truth. But such is not always the case, as this picture of Governor George Wallace flanked by me and Willie Nelson shows. The little boy in the picture, by the way, is my son, Shelton. (The Pelican C.B. Journal, Baton Rouge, La.)

Ajax Mountain, looking at its picture-postcard best. The tops of the peaks mark the Continental Divide. (Michael Bane)

Dick Willey and I work our way back up Ajax to the scene of the fall, at the very top of the snowfield in the center of the picture. (Michael Bane)

I landed near the foot of this snowfield. Both the rocks and I still have the scars. (Michael Bane)

From the top looking down—a long way down. (Michael Bane)

Me in my country—that's Idaho behind me; my toes are still in Montana.
(Michael Bane)

This is me after the fall, all rebuilt and patched back together. I don't think I look a bit the worse for wear.

Ole Waylon, one of the best friends I've ever had. (Michael Bane)

This is your basic wedding picture: bride, groom, family and all. Becky is, of course, the beautiful bride. (Michael Bane)

That's Becky's Louisiana "ya'll come back soon" smile. (Michael Bane)

would be the same. Essentially, what was happening was that one myth of Hank Williams was getting ready to overtake the other. By the time of the Cobo Hall show, the "Nashville Sound," with its sticky sweet strings and heavy orchestral arrangements, had just about shot its wad. Country music nationally was heading for a low ebb—college students were laughing at Merle Haggard doing "Okie From Muskogee," and the suburbs had become the last bastion of country music. As Bob Dylan put it, the times they were a-changin', and nobody was sure where it was finally going to lead.

Nobody, that is, except a group of singers and songwriters who had adopted the *other* myth of Hank Williams. While the Opry folks were still praising Daddy's name, sixteen years after his death, these young singers and songwriters had adopted a live fast, die young, and leave a beautiful corpse posture, and they talked about the way Hank did it.

But more than just posturing, they called for a return to the simplicity of Hank's music. People like Kris Kristofferson and Bobby Bare were proving that the Nashville Sound wasn't the only way to make country music, and in a few years even the hidebound Nashville establishment was going to take notice.

I think the reason I didn't take immediate notice was that I was working all the time. The road was still my life. All around me the country seemed to be falling apart. There were strikes and demonstrations against the war in Vietnam; there were race riots and marches by hard hats. And the only time such things touched on my world was when they intersected my path on the road. I had twenty-five shows canceled in 1968, and I almost got stuck in a riot in Newark, N.J. My own feelings were hard to explain. The music business was (and, in large respects, still is) a closed circle. What goes on outside is not nearly so important as what goes on inside that circle.

Politics? In 1968 I did some benefits for George Wallace because I didn't think the other candidates amounted to a nickel's worth of beans, certainly not when they talked about anything that had to do with the South. But when Martin Luther King was shot, one of my band members said something like, "Well, they finally got him. He sure stirred up enough trouble." All I could think about was Tee-Tot, the black man who taught Daddy to play the guitar and sing the blues. I thought a lot about the blues, maybe because it was something that clearly intersected my life, and I was ashamed of saying I lived in Tennessee.

16

So I married Sharon, my girlhood sweetheart and main woman-at-home, except that it wasn't that simple. Actually, I married Sharon in what amounts to a fit of pique, which would never have happened if it wasn't for the movie.

It wasn't enough that I was a superstar in country music—I needed to be a star of stage and screen as well. Elvis was in the movies; it was the least I could do.

And *Your Cheatin' Heart* had made everybody concerned, including me, buckets of money, so the producer, Sam Katzman, figured if the formula would work once, it would work again. After *Your Cheatin' Heart*, I was signed to a three-movie deal with MGM, and by the time I turned eighteen, the first movie was ready to go into production. Mother and various other people had hand-picked the script for me.

Basically, it was about a tobacco farmer who wanted to go to the big city and be a country music star. His family thinks he's crazy, but there's a loyal woman who sticks beside him through thick and thin, and there's a bunch of songs that'll make a great soundtrack

131

album, etc., etc. We didn't want to stray too far from the proven formula, and this movie, dubbed *A Time to Sing,* was about as close as we could come to making *Your Cheatin' Heart* again without going to Acuff-Rose for permission.

Not wanting to put all their eggs in my one, possibly frail, basket, MGM added Academy Award winner Ed Begley as my costar and Elvis movie veteran Shelly Fabares as the love interest. The marquee would read (they were very nervous about such things in Hollywood) "Starring Hank Williams Jr. and Ed Begley, With Shelly Fabares!" That was just fine with me, and I set up my schedule to go off the road for a few weeks to head for Hollywood and my future stardom.

Moviemaking just wasn't what it was cracked up to be. This wasn't any big-budget, ten-thousand-extras operation. We figured eighteen days of shooting, then I could head back on the road. When I got to the set, I was scared silly. I'd been studying the lines I was supposed to read for weeks, and I'd always thought of myself as a pretty fast study. But the moment I set foot on the set, I couldn't remember a darn thing.

"Don't worry about it, Hank," said Ed about two seconds after I arrived on the set. "Don't worry about the lines at all. All that shit's easy, once you understand the trick to it."

He leaned close and whispered conspiratorially. Don't memorize the whole page, he told me. "They're going to shoot the same two lines from *that* angle. Then they're going to shoot the same lines from *another* angle," he said. "By the time they get through, you'll know those two lines extremely well."

After a couple of days, it came to me that Ed was absolutely right, and then the whole operation settled into lots of fun. Ed Begley was a funny man, and he kept the set rolling in the aisles. That Hollywood crowd hadn't yet been inoculated against down-home country humor, either, and I was drawing my share of the laughs. In fact, I was having such a great time that I suggested to the powers-that-be that I bring Sharon Martin, my woman-at-home, out to the set so she could have a great time as well.

Boy, did that go over great.

An Autobiography

It was 1967, and not even Hollywood was all that enthused about having their eighteen-year-old boy wonder living in sin with his seventeen-year-old girlfriend, right there in public view. They could see ugly gossip items in every newspaper south of the Mason-Dixon Line, and the profits of *A Time to Sing* skyrocketing to zero.

Out of the question, they said.

Maybe I had a little bit of a swelled head, being eighteen and all, a star in country music and on my way to being a matinee idol. Plus Sharon and I had been getting *very, very,* friendly, and I was well on my way toward convincing myself I was wildly in love.

I want Sharon, I told the producers.

"Look, kid," they told me in their best Hollywood manners. "We're just not going to fly Miss So-And-So out here for you to play house with. It's just way outside the realm of possibility. Listen, we got a better idea. You want starlets? We'll get you starlets, bushels of starlets. Blondes, redheads, brunettes. Believe us, kid, it's better this way. Take a starlet. In fact, take two, they're small."

I crossed my arms, put my proverbial foot down, and went into a patented Tennessee sulk. I want my girlfriend.

Now they're getting mad. Listen, bumpkin, no girlfriend. Period. You wanna make a movie or you wanna moon over some broad? You can't do both, ace.

I was *furious*. Who did they think they were? Just some B-movie producers, while I was Hank Williams Junior, star of stage, screen, and what-have-you. I gritted my teeth and smiled. "Yes, sir," I said. "I understand, sir. Sorry to make such a fuss, sir." And they went away happy.

Just after midnight that same night, "Mr. Bill Forest" made nonstop reservations from Los Angeles to Nashville on the next available flight. Then "Mr. Bill Forest" called a cab, packed his bag, went straight to the airport, and caught his plane. The next morning, "Mr. Bill Forest" stepped off the plane in Nashville, called Sharon Martin, proposed, and Hank Williams Junior was married before the sun hit midday.

"That'll teach 'em," I thought.

133

I was sure I loved Sharon—as sure as any eighteen-year-old who was in love for the first time could be. And I was making my first real break from Mother, my first real decision as a man. What better decision could that be than to get married and to "settle down?"

Sharon and I settled down in my apartment in Nashville—nothing opulent, just your basic bachelor pad. A bed, lots of my guns and Civil War junk scattered around, a few guitars here and there. We'd had a honeymoon of about an afternoon when the phone rang. It was long distance from Hollywood.

"Get your butt back here right NOW!" the voice in the telephone shrieked. "Have you lost your goddammed hillbilly mind! We've got a contract!"

They were calling from the set of *A Time to Sing*, where everything was ready to go except for the star. They were angry. "You get your butt out here and finish this movie or we'll hang it out to dry!"

I just couldn't help grinning. I'd been waiting for this, and I wasn't a complete idiot. I'd talked to my attorney, and he'd given me a hand grenade to use.

"Your contract's not worth the paper it's written on," I said confidently. There was incoherent sputtering from the other end of the line. "When I signed that contract, I was seventeen years old. Think about that. I'm eighteen now, and I'm legally of age. When I signed the contract, I wasn't. Now what were you saying?"

There was dead silence. "We'll call you back," the voice said.

"Remember," I said before they could hang up, "I'm a married man now. I've got responsibilities! I don't have *time* to make your old movie."

I'm not sure, but I thought I heard a muffled curse before Hollywood hung up.

In a few hours the phone rang again.

"Hello, Mr. Williams," a different voice said. "We'd really like for you to come back out here and finish up *A Time to Sing*. We have a lovely house in Coldwater Canyon for you and your new bride, and we're planning to have a huge reception for you as soon as you get back. Of course, there's a pool and servants and whatever else you need. So when might we expect you on the set?"

"Give me a few days," I said magnanimously, "to get to know my bride, and we'll be on our way. And thank you for your courtesy."

They assured me that it was nothing, nothing at all.

The next week I was back in Hollywood, this time with Sharon, and things on the set were not quite as fun as they'd been before. But we had a great time, Sharon and I, playing around the house. In another week and a half we were finished, and at the cast party, the producers couldn't find enough praise for me. Never an acting lesson in his life, they said, and he did a fine job. Good natural actor, they said, and it made me feel great.

There were no more movies forthcoming, despite the three-movie contract. Privately, to some of my friends, the producers confirmed what they'd said at the cast parties. He's a natural talent, they said, and there's a great potential to become a really moving character actor. But, they said, relishing the thought even as they said it, "The little asshole's finished himself in Hollywood. Did he really think he could get away with that stunt? There won't be any more movies from MGM, ever!"

The studio issued me a check for $10,000, in my name instead of Mother's. I took it down to the biggest, ritziest Beverly Hills bank I could find, and I went in my Levi's and cowboy hat and boots.

"I'd like to cash this," I told the teller.

She looked at me for a long time, trying to figure out if I was going to hold up the bank, I guess, then she went to get a vice-president.

"Some kid here wants to cash a check," she said, passing the ten-grand check over. The honcho made a few phone calls and came back to the window.

"When were you born?" he asked.

I got that one right.

"Who was the producer of your picture?"

Right again. And on and on. It took forever. Finally the honcho sort of shrugged his shoulders and said, "How do you want it?"

"Cash, small bills."

"Are you absolutely sure of that?"

"Yep."

"All right. Give it to him."

I took the ten grand, unbuttoned my shirt, and stuffed it all down. Then I swaggered out of the bank, climbed into my ridiculous Nudie car that Mother had had ferried out to LA, and drove away into that Southern California sunshine. It was a glorious day!

I was doing a show in Springfield, Missouri, an old married man of three or four months, when I got the telegram:

"Time has a way of healing all things. Why not call me? Gwen."

There was a telephone number, and I felt that familiar feeling that had never really left creeping up on me. First, I started to throw the telegram away, since I was married and all, but I never got as far as wadding the darn thing up. I paced around the motel room about three times, then headed for the telephone. My palms were sweating when I heard that old familiar voice.

"Uh, Gwen . . . how're you doin'?"

"Oh, I'm doing just fine. And yourself?"

"Well, I got married . . ."

"So I read . . ."

"And, uh, maybe you'd like to see me again . . ."

It was amazing what that girl did to my resolve. Ten words, and I fell right back into it. Meet me in Wichita, I told her. I'm doing a show there in two days, and we can talk. If you can't get a flight, call back, and I'll charter you a plane. She agreed, and I hung up flushed with excitement, a flush that lasted about two minutes. "You damned fool," I thought to myself. "What are you trying to prove?"

The reunion in Wichita was all anyone could expect—love at second sight, or something like it. Before the evening was over, I was pledging eternal love to Gwen, ruing the day I ever met Sharon, much less married her, and setting up the dates for our next meeting. I still don't understand how I fell so far so fast. I don't suppose anyone really does. But I knew that the bottom line was I wanted it all. I wanted Sharon back at home; I wanted Gwen on the road; I wanted those other women-on-the-road to fill in the chinks when the other two weren't around.

So we got together with a vengeance, and pretty soon Gwen was meeting me at almost every date. What I did was charter airplanes for her, so we could get together as soon as possible. It all seemed so romantic—"Meet me in Podunk, Iowa, tomorrow afternoon. Hang the expense. I've got to see you," and blah, blah, blah. I spent a genuine fortune in airplane charter bills.

Of course, it couldn't go on. Gwen was, reasonably, I think, pushing for some kind of resolution. She'd meet me on the road, and before I'd know it, she'd be hysterical, and all my other pals would get upset. It can't go on like this, she'd say, and that was true, unless I bought an airline. Her or me, Gwen would say, and I'd beg the question. Then I'd go back to Nashville and be with Sharon, and everything would be different.

I liked Sharon a lot, and she loved me dearly. I didn't want to hurt her, but I couldn't shake Gwen off my mind. At first, I don't think Sharon realized anything was going on—she knew I was on the road constantly, and I think she'd accepted what that meant. Finally, though, it would have taken a blind man not to notice something was wrong. But Sharon took the brave course.

"Is it sex," she asked, "or does she mean something to you?"

Still backpedaling, I said sex. Sharon looked at me hard for a long time, then let me alone. From there, it went on for three or four months, sort of like a soap opera. I was living a cliché and didn't have sense enough to realize it.

Then one afternoon Sharon went grocery shopping, and something just snapped. As soon as she left the house, I started gathering up my clothes, my guns, my Civil War stuff, photographs,

137

things of Daddy's, and anything else that meant anything to me. Then I loaded them all into the back of my pickup truck. I was just crazy to get out of the house.

I hopped in the truck and headed to a friend's house, gave him the keys to the truck and told him to drive it somewhere and hide it. Then I asked him to drop me off at the airport, where I chartered a plane for Missouri. By the time Sharon got back from the store, I was already in Missouri in Gwen's arms. Sharon, who loved me, came back to an empty house, and her daddy had the long gone lonesome blues.

Boy, I thought, for once everything was going to be all right. It's hard to imagine how I could have been more wrong.

Probably the only good thing that came out of the whole experience came from the most unexpected direction—Hollywood. While I was *persona non grata* on the set of a picture, the word had gotten around that I did great movie soundtracks, and they were always looking for people to do great soundtracks. So I did a whole bunch of them, including *Kiowa Jones, Tick . . . Tick . . . Tick,* which was a very good movie in the vein of *In the Heat of the Night, Kelly's Heroes,* with Clint Eastwood, and a few other contributions here and there.

I even did a little television—worked up the pilots for a variety series, which definitely *wasn't* my forte, and did six weeks of a Florida music show called *Sun Country.* I liked that, but the viewing public didn't.

It was beginning to look like I was going to have to settle with being a country superstar. I hoped I could live with that.

17

Home!

It's time to go home!

As much as I love Montana, my heart leaped a little when the doctors said I could go back to Alabama. It's October, and it will still be autumn there, and I imagine how my cabin on the lake in Cullman will look. I can't wait.

The flight is uneventful. Mostly, I doze, and keep my stocking cap pulled down to my ears. I'm becoming a real afficionado of stocking caps—they do a great job of covering the hole still in my forehead, which is still months away from being patched.

As the plane gets closer, I get more and more nervous. What'll it be like? Will everything be the same? Will people still remember me?

I think it's a common fear among performers, especially performers who've been away for a while. Sure, I've resigned myself to never performing again. Sure, I can live with that. But there's a little voice that keeps gnawing away: Will they still know me? Will they still like me? Will they care?

Odd, those thoughts never occurred to me in the hospital in Missoula or even recovering at Dick and Betty's house. But the closer I get to Alabama, the more those old feelings start coming back.

We land in Huntsville and drive an hour to Cullman. God, it's good to see that place! The drive out to the lake takes another thirty minutes, and when we get to the cabin, it's all decked out in a "Welcome Back, Hank" banner, and it looks like Christmas. "Welcome home," says J. R. Smith. "Glad to have you back."

I go into the cabin and look around, and everything is almost the way I left it when I got the plane to Nashville and on to Montana. The cabin is an A-frame, very small, with a huge fireplace and warm brown carpeting. There's a deck out back, and it looks out over the pint-sized reservoir that serves Cullman. I sit down on the couch that looks out the window over the lake, underneath a huge painting of Daddy, and I feel a wave of peace settle over me. "I survived," I think incredulously. "I really made it."

I insist on spending at least one night at the cabin, but I know I still need someone to take care of me for a while. J. R. agrees to give me the one night, but he insists that the next morning I'm to move in with him and his family in downtown—such as it is—Cullman.

I sleep well that night, and I don't dream anything but good dreams.

The next day I'm adopted by a new family. Connie Smith, J. R.'s wife, gives me my own bedroom, and in no time at all I'm just one of the kids. Me and the other kids, Teressa, who's in her teens, Kellie, ten, and Alan, six, all get together in the afternoon to watch cartoons. I practice the guitar, just like in Montana, and I even try a little singing. Boy, it's awful! Once I get all my teeth in, though, I've got a feeling it's going to sound almost human.

"Maybe," I think . . . . "Just maybe." But I don't dare pursue the thought, not just yet.

Within a few weeks, though, it's time to go to Nashville and get my nine front teeth reinstalled, and I'm very excited about that. I want to bite something. I want to chew on an ear of corn or gnaw

140

up a steak bone. Shucks, I'd even settle for chomping down on a bunch of McDonald's french fries.

I go to my old family dentist in Nashville, who mourns the loss of my excellent teeth and all his years of work. Just what I wanted to hear. Then he takes a series of measurements and comes back looking like someone canceled Christmas.

"No way," he says. "I hate to say it, Hank, but your upper and lower jaws are just not lined up. I can't even think about putting in new teeth until those jaws are fixed. Go see an oral surgeon."

Damn! Somebody *has* canceled Christmas! At least for this year.

Why beat around the bush? On November 18 they haul me back into the hospital, this time to get my jaws *broken*. If I wasn't so depressed, I'd probably laugh about this—paying good money to have someone break my jaw. Jeez, I know people who'd do it for free.

On the table, cut the jaws loose, break the jaws, cut the upper septum all the way loose and line it up with the bottom, a little work on the nose, as long as they're in there, and a bit of straightening on the eye, although it's more along the line of patchwork rather than real repair, and again I wake up with my jaws wired together—again—*voilà* and a bladder infection.

After a week or so in the Nashville hospital, I head back to Alabama to spend Christmas drinking my turkey and dressing through a straw.

Which began sixteen months of reconstructive surgery, as the best doctors in the country labored to put Humpty Hank back together again. In a way, all the medical discomforts immediately after the fall were easier to bear—they were all concerned with the immediate problem of survival. And the answer came quickly. You lived or you died. The next year of operations was much, much harder on my soul and newfound resolve, simply because there was so much time involved. I wanted to be made whole—well, as whole as possible—and I wanted it done yesterday. The day before, if possible.

But I had to wait, and I cautioned myself to be patient. I looked inside myself to find the strength, and I prayed for more strength. "Give me a sign, Lord," I prayed. "Help me." And I waited.

The new wires came out of my jaws in January, and I was amazed at how adept I'd become at eating through a straw. Steak and taters, yum, slurp 'em down. My jaws lined up properly, and I was fitted with a set of temporary plastic plates, which had the annoying habit of falling out whenever I bit into something—especially hot dogs. It seemed like I was always having hot dogs with relish, catsup, mustard, and plastic teeth. With the plates came not only the great sensation of taking a chomp out of something, but the more difficult task of learning how to talk all over again.

What I'd been doing was mouthing words as best I could. My mouth, especially the roof of my mouth, where all the "t" and "th" sounds are made, was a mass of stitches, and as those stitches came out and the permanent repair work went in, I found I sounded like a little baby.

"Gimme dis," I'd say. "Whadda we gonna haav toniite for super?" Something like that.

It was important to learn to talk, because if I couldn't talk, I couldn't sing, and I found I wanted to sing very badly, which amazed me. Because what I was was an entertainer. Where I wanted to be was on stage.

I'd like to say that the idea of going back on stage exploded into my mind, after some significant event. I'd like to say that I looked to the sky, and it lit up like neon, saying "HANK WILLIAMS JUNIOR! SING!" But nothing like that happened. Instead, the idea just sort of crept into my mind, a little bit at a time. There was no big decision to be made. I was a performer, and the only question left was "when?"

Somewhat grimly I set about learning how to talk. I practiced my vowels. I practiced forming words with my mouth. I practiced singing. I talked on the CB radio all the time, to anyone who'd listen. By the time they finished putting in my permanent teeth and capping all the others that'd been shattered by the fall, I knew I

142

could do it. Don't ask me how—a lot of people still had their doubts, but somewhere in the center of me I knew I could walk on stage and sing.

"Thanks again," I prayed silently. "Thanks."

In March I went back to Montana for the touchiest surgery of all—doing something about the gaping hole in my forehead. Dr. Dewey offered me no illusions. He'd lost one patient, a little girl, during exactly the same type of surgery. The operation was to insert a plastic plate into my forehead to cover the exposed portion of my brain.

As it was, you could see every heartbeat, every course of fluid through my brain. It looked terrible, and was terrifically dangerous. Someone could have, literally, poked a finger into my brain. Dr. Dewey's plan was to do a minimum of cutting, whenever possible cutting through the old scars to cut down on future plastic surgery. He'd then smooth the remaining jagged edges of bone, insert a wire mesh, and cover the mesh with quick-setting surgical plastic, something like the way a plasterer will repair a wall.

He pulled it off brilliantly, and, happily, my body didn't reject the plastic section—something the doctors had been quite worried about. Had there been a rejection, the operation would have had to be repeated with a steel plate, with the possibility of having no protection over that section of the brain at all.

Within a few days, though, I was on my way back to Alabama.

The operations seem to run together in my mind, and it's hard to separate one from the other. The trick, like the trick Ed Begley had showed me on the set of *A Time to Sing,* was to not worry so much about the overall thing, just concentrate on the bits and pieces. I never thought about the operations themselves, and it used to drive J. R. crazy. Once, when I was being wheeled into surgery here or there, I reminded J. R. to stop by a gun store and make a deposit on an antique revolver I'd found the week before.

"Jesus, Hank," J. R. almost shouted. "How can you think about something like that at a time like this!"

"J. R.," I told him, "how can I think about anything else?"

One thing that helped was that after each operation I was demonstrably better, which does wonders for keeping your spirits up. The last really major operations were in Charlottesville, Virginia, and they had to be booked a full year in advance. The surgeons there were the best in the country for the orbit of the eye, and they were going to "adjust" my eyes.

Adjust is a mild word for what they did. They were going to have to rebuild my cheek, build up a side of my nose, anchor the socket of my eye to the new construction work (sometimes I tend to think of myself as a building under construction), align my eyeball, and make sure everything worked.

In November, a year and three months after the fall, we did exactly that. Imagine your eyes as two lenses. One of my lenses was in the wrong place, and they first pushed it in, then later pulled it back out, until they got the right eye pretty well lined up with the left. I was in Virginia a week, then I headed for Idaho to go mountain lion hunting. Unfortunately, the wire that held the right side of my face together broke, and the plastic construction that was my cheek rotated *up*, taking my eye with it.

It didn't hurt. But boy it looked like holy hell. It was red and swollen and ugly and I looked like some kind of demon.

"Finish your hunt," the doctors in Virginia told me. "Then get yourself back up here."

I got my lion, then the folks in Virginia readjusted my plastic superstructure. I was lying in the hospital in Virginia when I heard a familiar voice out in the hall. The only visitors I was allowed was my family, and the unmistakable voice of Merle Kilgore was literally echoing through the hospital hallways.

"Who am I!" the voice said. "I'm only his brother, that's who I am! Let me in that room!" What nurse could stand in his way?

So Merle lurched into my hospital room, and I could see right off that he was, shall we say, into the cups just a tiny bit.

"Hank!" he boomed. "Howya doin, boy?"

"Just great," I said. "And yourself?"

"Well, Hank," said Merle, looking for all the world like a tur-

144

quoise cowboy nightmare. "I hate to ask, being that you're sick and all, but would you mind too very much if I laid down in your hospital bed? I'm feeling poorly."

Well. I gathered up my IV, wrapped my robe around me, and sat down in the chair next to the bed. Merle climbed into the bed like the Jolly Green Giant toppling over. His bus driver, who'd come in with him, lay down on the floor at the foot of the bed like an obedient puppy.

"Much obliged, Hank," Merle said, about two seconds before he went to sleep.

Then everybody but me was snoring away, and not even the nurses had the heart to dump that giant out of bed.

"Now that," I thought, "is a true friend!"

18

Slippin' Around

Sometimes it's hard to put your finger on exactly when you crest a hill and start on the downslope. You'll be going up and up and up, then things'll start leveling off, and you'll think you're on flat ground for a while. But before you can even realize what's happening, you're going down, and the grade gets steeper and steeper until you're totally out of control.

I never even saw the crest of the hill coming, and I didn't know I was on the way down until I was just about ready to hit bottom. All I knew when I got on that airplane in Missouri was that I was getting ready to have everything I wanted, at least, everything I wanted at the time. It's amazing how a person can be so wrong.

My life started to take on all the aspects of a bad country song—the divorce was slow in coming, and Sharon, rightfully, I think, was going for blood. For most of the time, I was sharing an apartment in Nashville with Kilgore—there were two bedrooms; Kilgore had one and Gwen and I had the other. But it wasn't that simple. There were private detectives dogging my every step, trying to see if I was living in sin with another woman. Since I was dogging the private eyes, it became a big game.

I bought cars like a madman, and as soon as Sharon spotted me in one, I'd trade it in. Buy a yellow Lincoln, trade it for a white Cadillac. Buy a Volkswagen, trade it for a Ford. Every time I did it I lost a heap of money, and some used car dealer in Nashville was raking it in. I had my green-and-white Ford pickup truck painted, then I'd have to run to the courthouse and think of some hare-brained excuse to get the license plate changed. Even that didn't work for very long.

So I took to wearing different-colored wigs as well as changing my car every week. I'd slip out the back way, dive into a friend's car, and have him cruise all over Nashville while I changed clothes and hair. Then he'd let me off at a secret parking place and I'd hop into my new car, pick up Gwen, and off we'd go, laughing like we'd just pulled off the Brink's job.

It stopped being funny, though, the day I got busted.

I'd gone to a baseball game and was feeling pretty good. So good, in fact, that I'd decided to spend the evening writing some new songs—something I'd been neglecting for more than a little while. There was the proverbial knock on the door.

"Police. Open up!"

I looked over at Kilgore, who looked as innocent as a newborn babe. I was still trying to figure out what Merle had done to bring down the law on us when I opened the door.

"Randall Hank Williams, Junior?"

"That's me." Oh, shit.

"We've got a warrant for your arrest, Mr. Williams. We've also got a warrant to search your apartment. If you'll just step over to the side and let the officer search you."

"What in the hell is going on! I haven't done anything! What's the warrant for, anyway?" My toe, which I'd managed to bust up playing ball and which had been quiescent all evening while I was writing, started throbbing like a blinking light. I was so mad my ears must have been flashing off and on red.

"Cohabitation, Mr. Williams."

"Cohabitation! What in the hell are you talking about?"

148

"We have information that you are living with a woman who is not your wife. Under Tennessee state law, that is illegal. Now, if you'll just stand back while we search the apartment, things will go a lot easier on you."

"Look around here and see if you can find a woman. . . ." Thank God Gwen had gone back to Missouri for a while. She'd even taken all her clothing. ". . . Be sure to look under the couch, cousin, in case I've got her stashed under there."

One officer came running back out of my bedroom with a black leather jacket. The officers examined it and held it up to me.

"If there's no woman here, how do you explain this?" the officer said.

"It's my motorcycle jacket, damn it," I said, and the heck of it was that it *was* my motorcycle jacket. "It gets cold on a motorcycle, and they've got to fit tight."

They didn't say anything else, then somebody shouted, "Oh my God, he's got a gun!." And a roomful of cops went for their pieces. If I hadn't been so scared, I would have probably broken out laughing.

"And I've got a permit for the damn thing, too!" I shouted over the general hubbub.

But off we went to jail. I was fuming. They fingerprinted me, took my picture, all the time with me ranting about my rights, my wife, and woman's liberation, which all seemed to go in together. Then they hauled me in front of a judge, who asked how I chose to plead to the charge. "Not guilty!" I shouted at about volume ten, and my lawyers, who'd all hotfooted it down there after my one complimentary phone call, clucked around the bench like mother hens.

The judge listened to my story, asked the arresting officers if there had indeed been a woman present at my address, then asked me to stand.

"Son," the judge said, "I don't blame you for shouting not guilty. I concur. Case dismissed."

It wasn't so much fun after that. Just like it wasn't so much fun when I was thoroughly searched going through customs in Bermuda, where I'd been booked for a couple of shows. Customs had been tipped that I'd be carrying drugs. I wasn't.

Gwen met me in Bermuda, and after the initial irritation of the customs deal had worn off, we had a good time. Such a good time that we got to see the whole thing again in living color and with sound effects at the divorce proceedings a few months later. Interesting pictures. Hell of a soundtrack. Sharon got $90,000 cash, alimony, the $100,000 house, a new Cadillac and some other nickels and dimes. She also found my pickup truck that I'd asked my friend to hide, and she'd sold my entire gun collection, which was worth thousands and thousands of dollars. All settled nicely and neatly out of court, so the Hank Junior on the Beach dirty movie didn't end up on the public record.

After an appropriate time, say three or four minutes, Gwen and I were married, and we had a son, whom we named Shelton, after my grandfather. I was happy—at least, I sure thought I was.

With all the personal goings-on, one might get the impression that my career had shifted from high into, say, neutral. One might be right. My energies were all being channeled into the C & W soap opera my personal life had become, and going on stage had become almost a waste of my precious time.

I mean, after all, I was on top, why should I go out there and work? Heck, I didn't even have money as an excuse. When I turned eighteen, I started receiving one half of Daddy's royalties, and they were substantial. I used to joke about it, even. If I wanted to, I told my friends, the hardest work I ever had to do was walk to the mailbox and then go cash the check. What I'm doing on my own was just *gravy*. Say every year I made $125,000 in royalty money, which was a pretty fair figure. So who has to work?

Besides, a lot of water had flowed under the bridge since Cobo Hall, and not all of it was good water. Sure, I could go out there on stage and play a dozen instruments and run around the stage like a dervish, and that'd get me applause. Or I could stand in one place and sing Daddy's songs, and that'd get me even more applause.

150

Standing ovations, even. And running around the stage took a lot of energy, which was being channeled elsewhere. It was easier to sing *Your Cheatin' Heart.*

While I was running around Nashville dodging shamuses, my audience was busy changing. The pigeons were coming home to roost, and the changes that had begun with the underground myth of Daddy and become entrenched in the late 1960s were shaking Nashville with a vengeance.

They were good changes—for Nashville. Country music was on the upswing. But the smart money was already saying that it was never going to be business as usual again in Music City, and I was just too involved with my own problems to even see it coming.

A whole new breed of country singers was coming up, and they were the people who would bring country music to the attention of the whole nation. They were people like Loretta Lynn and Tammy Wynette, Dolly Parton and Willie Nelson, Waylon Jennings and Johnny Paycheck. I'd even worked with most of them at one time or the other, usually with me as the headliner and them as one of the package acts. Waylon was even on one of my mother's Caravans of Stars, and he got about fifteenth billing: "And also, we guess, Waylon Jennings. . . ." But these new acts were coming on strong, and they were dominating the charts with their music. If I had to define that music now, I'd have to say it was more honest than the music we'd been singing. It captured their personal tragedies and the daily trials in their lives. It reassured the audience that they were somebodies, all important. Like Daddy's music.

Only I'd been singing Daddy's songs almost every night for the past fifteen or sixteen years and I thought I knew everything there was to know about them. What I'd forgotten, and what those other singers had finally remembered, was that knowing is not the same as feeling. I thought I knew my father, but I had let his soul slip away from me, and a lot of other people had found it.

There was a new sound coming out of the South. It came from people like Charlie Daniels and the Allman Brothers Band, and it owed a debt to not only country but to blues as well. Well, that doesn't actually tell the whole picture. Country music has always had a debt to the blues, to black music, that country has never wanted to acknowledge. The real guts of country, the real guts of Daddy's music, I think, came from that black tradition, both blues and gospel. But by the early 1970s, the country music establishment had succeeded in scouring country music of any black influence—can't take a chance on confusing country with rock and roll, they said.

What the Allman Brothers and Charlie Daniels and the Marshall Tucker Band said was, to hell with that. We're not afraid to rock and roll and still sound country. Most people in Nashville went to great lengths to ignore this new voice from the South, but the first time I heard it my ears perked up. "These guys," I thought, "are really doing something. These guys are growing, and they're taking the music with them." Sure, nobody ever thought of the Allman Brothers as a country group when they got started, but that was more a function of the times than anything else. Hippies didn't listen to country music, and country people didn't have no truck with that rock and roll.

It sounds so silly now, but in the early 1970s those words couldn't have been any truer if they'd have been carved on marble and handed down from Lookout Mountain in Chattanooga. That was the *gospel* truth! If you listened to country music, you were a redneck asshole, and if you listened to rock and roll, you were a hippie freak. They were polarized times, and the music was (and still is) the cutting edge of the times. So what happened to the Allman Brothers in Macon, Georgia, was of no concern to the pickers in Nashville, Tennessee, a couple of hundred miles up the road. But it was important to *me*, because those Georgia boys were trying to tell me something, only I didn't quite have the time to sit down and figure out what.

I'd always wanted to rock and roll. When I was a kid, I'd even released a couple of straight rock and roll songs (one, "Meter Reader Maid," released on a different label, Verve, under a "different" name, Bo Cephus), but there was something more at stake here. It wasn't just a question of "Hank Williams Junior wants to

152

rock.'' The music was changing, and every once in a while I had a gut feeling that I wanted to be a part of that change—no, that I wanted to be at the *forefront* of that change.

But when I got up there on stage, there just weren't any kids in the audience who were interested about hearing the music change. In fact, there weren't any kids in the audience at all. Somewhere between 1968 and 1971, I'd lost all the kids my age. I'd stand up there on stage and look out over a sea of people who were Daddy's age and who wanted to hear Daddy's songs. My peers were off listening to Charlie Daniels or secretly grooving on Waylon Jennings.

I didn't make that connection until years later. All I knew is that the kids had gone away, and maybe I'd better stick to the tried and true material. I didn't really have time to think about it, because I was still having a real good time. I had my friends around me, and I had my new wife who was beautiful and all a man could ever want, and I had a son.

I loved them both more than I loved my music. Maybe that was part of the problem.

What I didn't realize was that the good times were already rolling downhill, and the grade was getting steeper and steeper.

Something was wrong between Gwen and me, something that I was at a loss to identify, much less correct. The ice wasn't melting. Gwen didn't seem to care whether I went on the road or not. Go, stay, who gives a damn? I begged her to go with me, and she shrugged it off. Why?

Fire your manager, she told me. The new girl in the office is a bitch. I quit. I would have done anything to make things go right again.

Maybe if I really loved her I'd take her to Vegas. Maybe if I did more of Daddy's songs on stage people wouldn't scowl and come backstage afterwards and call me half the man my daddy was. And maybe . . . maybe . . . maybe . . . maybe if I'd had my eyes a little wider open, I'd have seen the roof when it started to cave in on top of me.

And so we started down.

19

Hank's Ghost

In the beginning there was the Word, and the Word was Jim Beam. James B. Beam Distilling Company, makers of fine Kentucky bourbon whiskey. Aged for years in wooden barrels in Clermont/Beam, Kentucky, just waiting for Hank Williams Junior to send out the call for help. And Lord, I called.

"The thing is this, Hank, I just don't want to be married any more," Gwen was saying, and that was just what I needed. No, actually, what I needed most of all was sleep. I was up to almost 250 show dates a year, gone every two days out of three, which doesn't count my recording commitments, guaranteed to eat up at *least* another month or six weeks. Besides, I'd already heard this lecture last week. Or maybe the week before.

"There has to be more in life than just sitting home waiting for some damn country singer to come in off the road," she said, and she meant it. "I want more out of life than waiting on you hand and foot!"

"You could come with me." I was getting pissed. "You came with me on the road before Shelton was born. You sure as hell came with me on the road *before* we were married!"

155

"You think things are going to be any better if I do go with you? You think things are going to be any better for *me*?" She was spitting fire and brimstone, and God help me, but I loved her. "Don't you understand even a little bit? I am a person, a whole, complete person. I am not a secondary part of Hank Williams Junior. You go ahead and laugh all you want, but I want to be *free*. I want my own money. I want my own job—I was a model once, remember? I could be an actress. I could be a lot of things other than a good little wifey, sitting at home and waiting. Can't you understand that even a little?"

What the hell was I supposed to see? She'd chased me for years, all the way through one marriage and finally into another one with her. Now that she had me, all she wanted to do was bitch. That's the way I saw it, and it's possible that I was wrong.

"Oh, Hank, don't you see? You only come home once a week, and then all you want to do is screw and sleep. There's got to be more in my life than that!"

I responded the only way I knew how. I grabbed my jacket, stormed out the door, and headed for the first bar I could lay my hands on. Sometimes you don't realize how true country songs are until you find yourself in the middle of one.

The Jim Beam eased the pain, and I didn't know what else to do. I loved her, but I didn't understand her. I honest-to-God didn't know what she wanted, because all my life women seemed to fall into neat categories.

There was something I learned while I was obsessed with the Civil War: The battle isn't always to the bravest or the swiftest or the best prepared. Everything can be going your way, and it looks like there's nothing that can stop you. Then your horse stumbles in a gopher hole, and it's all over. Just like that. My life, my career, were a juggernaut. Rocket to stardom, guaranteed, and I'd put one foot in front of the other without really giving it much thought as to why. Too many of the questions in my life had been answered "because," and I'd accepted that answer maybe one time too many.

My relationship with Gwen was based on two props: I had an

idealized vision in my mind of How Life Should Be. Given who I was and what I was, I should have so-and-so. A wife and a child, for instance. An adoring audience. Bigger and better records each year. Unconsciously, I held to that ideal—things got better all the time. They'd *always* gotten better, so why should they not? And to the best of knowing my own mind, I loved her. I wanted to share my life; I wanted her to be a part of my life. I couldn't believe she'd want otherwise.

Things refused to get better between Gwen and me. Instead, they got worse.

One day when I came off the road she wouldn't let me touch her. It didn't feel "right," she said. Maybe if I could sleep downstairs for a few days it would be better for both of us. I slept downstairs, and it wasn't better. At least not for me. The evenings went a lot easier if I spent a little time with the Jim Beam before I started home. So much better, in fact, that it became harder and harder to even conceive of a time when I *didn't* need the bottle to face a night with my wife.

We tried marriage counselors, which a lot of my "friends" thought was a real laugh. "Look at ole Hank," they'd say. "We bet your daddy would have never gone to no counselors." We went to psychologists, together and separately. We tried group sessions. We tried anything to make the marriage work.

They all told us exactly the same thing: Forget it. There's nothing there worth saving.

I would be damned if I believed that!

I remember one guy especially, sitting there behind his smug little desk in his smug little college graduate suit. "There is no such thing as pain," he told us, he told me. "There is only the *fear* of pain." The bastard looked so smug. He was still looking smug when I stormed out of the room, slammed his door, and headed for a bar.

You want to know about pain? Pain is watching the one thing in your life that you want to succeed fail. Pain is having your own private apartment in your own home, because your wife can't stand to sleep with you, much less have sex. Nice bachelor pad, right there off your living room. Pain is watching your wife have an affair with another man, then going out and having one of your own so you can show her. Pain is watching that bottle of Jim Beam creep toward the bottom and still not being able to flush the whole damn thing out of your mind.

And pain is walking out on that stage, two nights out of every three, with your insides all knotted into a ball, and singing songs to a crowd who didn't appreciate whether you lived or died. They were assholes, the audience, and I wonder why I'd never seen that before. They were bloodsuckers, just like ninety-nine percent of the people I dealt with every day. All they wanted was their private piece of Hank Williams, Junior, and they didn't give a good God-damned what happened to me after they got their chunk. Just like my new manager, Buddy Lee. Just like my record company. Just like my mother. And just like my wife.

I didn't want to believe that. I'd stand backstage and look out at that audience, and I'd pray that Gwen really loved me, and that it would all work out. And then I'd stand there and cry, and the tears would drip down on my fancy Nudie suit, and Jerry Rivers, who was in my band and Daddy's band as well, would stand to the side and wring his hands. He'd seen all this once before, and he knew where it led.

At home, Gwen read another of the reports from the shrinks.

"Well, this one says I'm not much of a person," she read, pouring herself a drink. "I don't really love anybody, it says here. I'm a lost cause and I'm having an affair. Well, God damn them all!"

Maybe, she said, we should get a divorce. Followed by a shocked silence and a lot of crying on both our parts. No divorce, at least not yet.

Maybe we should not get a divorce and live apart for a while. A separation, only that wouldn't look so good to the public and all. We compromised, and fixed up the apartment downstairs into a complete living unit rather than just a bed. I lived there. We didn't share meals or beds or even the same friends. All we shared was the same address and last name. For all her talk, we didn't share the bills, either, and there seemed to be more and more of them every day. I wasn't starving—in 1970 I'd signed the biggest contract in the history of MGM Records, guaranteeing me $500,000 a year, not counting what I made touring or the royalties from Daddy's estate. That adds up to a lot of nickels and dimes. But you'd be amazed about how fast those nickels and dimes got spent. Thrift has never been my strong point, and it sure as heck wasn't Gwen's! So maybe, as soon as I can get a little time off the road, I can head for Africa on safari. I begged Gwen to go with me, but she'd have no part of it. You want to go crawl around a jungle, that's your business, she said. Try not to get killed by some animal that's smarter than you are.

I bought guns and cars like they were going out of style, and Gwen bought clothes like the department stores in Nashville and points east were going to close tomorrow. I didn't bother with my taxes, because I had accountants that were supposed to take care of that sort of thing. That's why I had a manager. When my friends needed money, I gave it to them. When we went somewhere, ole Hank paid, and we all traveled first class. See how happy I am, I told the world, you can tell by the way I throw all this money around. God damn I'm a cheery fellow! Then I'd go home to my "apartment" for just long enough to feel so sick inside I could throw up. When I'd stood it for as long as I could, I'd go looking for Jim Beam.

He wasn't hard to find.

Neither were the drugs, once I knew where to look. Maybe take a couple of Valiums or Darvons, followed by a good stiff swig of whiskey, give it about fifteen or twenty minutes, and the whole world, Gwen included, took on a rosy glow, and pretty soon I started to see what Daddy and Cash and Kilgore saw in this stuff. With liquor you'd always have to face that inevitable morning after, with your mouth feeling like used steel wool and your temples trying to figure out a way to get off your head. With pills, though, you could postpone that morning after for a hell of a long time, weeks, in fact. You could play them shows all night if you had to, then spend the whole next day pretending you were the happy man and wife, then play all night again, and you'd be none the worse for wear.

But the audiences noticed. They noticed when I hit the wrong notes on my banjo. They noticed when my piano playing started sounding like a four-year-old's. They noticed when I had to close my eyes and hang on to the microphone stand for dear life, while the dope and the whiskey tried to come to an agreement behind my eyes. They noticed when I screwed up Daddy's songs, and they weren't mumbling nice things when they walked out.

Once, I was backstage after a particularly bad show, and I was still oh-so stoned, when this girl came backstage. I figured her for a groupie, and felt that familiar rise, but all she did was just walk up to me and stare. After she stared awhile, she just walked away.

"You aren't half the man your father was," she said. "And you never will be."

Just like that. And, oh Lord, at that moment I knew she was right. I had failed.

There was nothing to do but hide deeper and deeper in whiskey and pills, with the sincere hope that I could find a point that was so low I could never get out again. There didn't seem to be any place to turn. Mother's health was already failing, and every time I hit that bottle, all she could see was the ghost of Daddy, getting ready to leave her alone. Gwen was perfectly happy to go to all the parties and travel around the country as Mrs. Hank Williams Junior, sometimes with other friends, both male and female, sometimes alone. I definitely wasn't needed there.

All of a sudden I didn't have any friends that amounted to anything, with a few exceptions—Kilgore and Cash, both of whom had gone through similar problems of their own. The rest just kind of blended into the background, content to wait and watch to see if I was really going to follow Daddy's footsteps all the way to the grave. My friends . . . just waiting to lay me on a slab, so they could all say they knew me back when. Bitter? You don't know the meaning of the word.

The only person I felt close to was Daddy, and he was dead. I understood him now like I never understood him before. I understood his pain, and I understood his genius. I also understood that there was really no hope for me, either. I had walked the path this far, and I had to take it to the end.

Ironically, I was writing some of my best music ever—"Last Love Song," "Before You Fell Out of Love With Me," "Getting Over You." Hit songs. And, in the studio, I was singing the blues better than ever. Every once in a while. "Rainy Night in Georgia," "Eleven Roses" ("Look in the mirror . . . The twelfth rose is you . . ."). Ask any songwriter, the lower you get, the better you work. You really want to know how to play and write that hurtin' music, the answer is real simple—hurt for a while.

People were buying the records, but they didn't like what they saw at the concerts. They didn't like what they heard whispered in gossip, that I was headed for the same cold dead end as my Daddy. They looked up there on that stage, and they saw a man haunted by some demon with a ghost standing at his elbow, and they acted pretty much like my friends.

It seemed that nobody wanted to be around for the end.

The years all run together—'71, '72, '73, '74. An endless nightmare of bars and shows, of sick mornings and stoned nights and big chunks of time where there are no memories at all. Of Jim Beam and cheery, multicolored pills, and strange girls with vacant eyes. I remember sitting down at the dining room table with $10,000 in cash and finding that it didn't even begin to touch my bills. Wrecked cars and warnings from sheriffs who knew my daddy. A birthday party for Shelton with balloons stuck all over the ceiling, and I think I was home for almost a week. Gwen working on a small part in a movie with Burt Reynolds, and coming home from Hollywood all tan and beautiful. She had a new dress, and I remember you could see her nipples hard through the dress, and it made me want her so bad. Only she had to rest up for her part, and not tonight, dear. Not any night, dear. She had other friends. I had my bottles.

And like the Lefty Frizzell song, of the same name, I never went around mirrors, 'cause I didn't know who'd be looking out at me.

20

The Cold, Cold Heart

The gas gauge on my hotrod Ford truck was looking pretty thirsty, so I started throttling it down and looking for the next exit along that Christmas-ribbon concrete slab of Interstate 40. I was depressed, so I was fighting it the only way I knew how—I'd bought the most incredible truck money could buy, and now I was going to Paris, Tennessee, to go hunting.

Gwen and I were finished—we were even ready to scrap the façade we'd been living for the last two years. She'd filed for a divorce once and changed her mind, and now she was getting ready to file again in earnest. I was the hottest gossip item in Nashville: "Hank Williams Junior, living fast and loose like his old man, was seen around the town with Miss So-And-So. The lovely Mrs. Williams had no comment." The bloodsuckers. I hadn't trusted the press ever since the *National Enquirer* quoted me as saying my music was better than Daddy's. What I'd really said was that recording techniques were better today than they were in Daddy's time. The bastards.

People were starting to come to my shows to see if I would fall off stage. Heck, my mental life was starting to be a public event, sort of like the lions and Christians in the arena. For a measly five bucks you could step right up and see whether the son of the greatest country artist of all time could get through his set without dropping a guitar or forgetting the words to "Cold, Cold Heart." You think ole Hank could give 'em a show a couple of years ago, you ought to see him now . . .

The bastards.

So I bought the truck, and that made me feel better. It was a killer truck! The biggest engine I could get Ford to stuff in it when money was no object. Special transmission, special fuel pump, special exhaust system, special carburetors—damn shame I couldn't get a rocket assist or something—and that mother would fly! I'd get out there on Interstate 65, south of Nashville, and just wind it up and up and up until that speedometer was reading 100 . . . 120 . . . 130 . . . I swear that truck would do 160 miles an hour, and I loved to hear that sumbitch engine roar. Made me feel immeasurably better about the world.

But it was running out of gas, damn it, and I started looking for an exit. I listened to the big ole engine slow its rumble, and pulled off at the next exit. Clarksville, Tennessee. The center of the civilized universe. The first gas pump I saw was at one of the general store-type deals, with gas, groceries, plate lunches, and a bar, all packed into a place about the size of an average living room.

I shut off the truck, being careful to reach down and turn off the electric fuel pump—that took some getting used to. Worked like a bandit, but you had to remember to shut the damn thing on and off. I told the old man to fill it up with rocket fuel, as premium as he could get it, and then headed for the bar. So maybe I'd had a little to drink, but I went into that second-rate honky-tonk with the idea of getting a little more. I ordered a shot of Jim Beam and headed for the jukebox.

I'm a total jukebox addict. I can't look at one without feeding the darn thing every single quarter I've got in my pocket. Maybe I just don't like it when things get too quiet.

So I waltzed up to that jukebox like I owned the place, which I probably could have done for the change I had in my pocket. I dropped my quarter down the slot and started looking. What I found was my ghost, my inspiration, my daddy, this time in the form of Linda Ronstadt singing "I Can't Help It If I'm Still in Love With You." I played that, took my drink, and headed back to my seat.

> Today I passed you on the street
> And my heart fell at your feet
> I can't help it if I'm still in love with you
> Somebody else was at your side
> And she looked so satisfied
> I can't help it if I'm still in love with you . . .

And I was crying, sobbing my eyes out. I couldn't even begin to control it—huge, racking sobs that caused the bartender to stop what he was doing and stare and whatever other patrons there were to sidle over toward the door. The tears just kept falling on the table, and Linda just kept on singing Daddy's song.

> It's hard to know another's lips will kiss you
> And hold you just the way I used to do
> Heaven knows how much I really miss you
> I can't help it if I'm still in love with you.

It was like Daddy reachin' out across the years, telling me he understood. I paid for my drink with tears in my eyes and went back out to the truck.

The Goddamned thing wouldn't start!

I threatened it and cajoled it and kicked the son-of-a-bitch, and that engine just ground and ground and ground without firing a single time. I finally got out, pushed the truck away from the pumps, and went back for another drink. I'd start the drink, get pissed all over again, and go back out and work on the truck. No dice.

"Great," I thought. "Just great. It's the middle of the night and I'm in Clarksville, Tennessee, blubbering like an idiot and kicking a truck that won't start."

To put it mildly, I felt like sheer, unadulterated hell. What I had to do was write a song. It was sort of like writing "Standing in the Shadows," so long ago. Like being touched by some kind of C & W muse.

I went out to the truck, got a pencil and paper, and sat down on the seat to start writing. All in all, it took about ten minutes, and the sun was coming up when I finished:

> As long as I can keep a lot of friends around me,
> Aw, it helps to keep a worried mind occupied.
> I do all right until dark of night surrounds me,
> And then I think of her, and then I cry.
> Lord, it's dawn and I'm still here stoned at the jukebox,
> Playing "I can't help it if I'm still in love with you . . ."
> 'Cause that's the kind of songs it takes to get that old hurtin' out.
> And Lord, I love that hurtin' music,
> 'Cause I am hurtin' too!

The words just flew out of my mind; the song was there, fully formed, and all I needed to do was copy it down. The service station owners were sure I'd lost my mind. Maybe they were right.

> I've been running up and down old Interstate 65.
> I loved a Nashville, Tennessee, woman, Lord, how I tried!
> Now I'm busted stone flat down in Huntsville. [*I liked that better than Clarksville*]
>
> I've got nothing but time and bottles to kill
> And I never thought I could be like that!
> Lord it's the cold hard morning and I'm stoned at the jukebox . . .

I felt almost human again. I stuffed the paper into the glove compartment, and in the light of dawn I could see the cab of the truck pretty well. I saw the switch on the electric fuel pump. It was in the "off" position. I'd never turned it back on.

I slid across the seat, hit the switch, and the truck started right up. I was almost smiling when I hit the Interstate.

I wasn't smiling for very long. I'd heard all the whispers about

166

the "Williams Curse," and I wasn't even laughing a little bit. Mostly I was crying. I'd buy a bottle of Jim Beam or, for a little variety, Jack Daniel's—I tried to stick to sourmash whiskey; God knows why—go back to my little apartment and haul out the stereo. Then I'd put on one of Daddy's records and cry my eyes out.

"You knew," I'd say to the record player. "You knew all along, damn it!"

"Why can't I free your doubtful mind, and melt your cold, cold heart?" the record player would reply. Then I'd cry some more and drink some more.

"I know why you died, Daddy," I'd say. "I understand. It's so lonely! I wish I'd really known you, Daddy. We'd understand each other. How can we love women so much and they not care about us? Why is our life so lonely?"

"Oh, the blues come around. Yes, the blues come around," the record player replied. "Every evening when the sun goes down . . ."

And I'd drink and cry until I was too drunk to drink any more, then I'd pass out.

Self-pity's a tricky beast, and the trickiest thing about it is that it's like a self-fulfilling prophecy. I couldn't cope with losing Gwen because it upset the balance of my life, and I'd never realized for a second how delicate that balance was.

Just as importantly, I'd never realized how deeply ingrained my daddy's myth really was. It was so ingrained that, somehow, it seemed *right* that my life should fall apart. Morbid? Hell, yes! But how many times can a person be told he's the reincarnation of someone else until he finally starts believing it in earnest? Now, at twenty-five years old, I was more like him than I ever figured I'd be—drunk, on dope, divorced, and well on my way to being a laughing stock. I was also a star.

Even while the spiral of self-pity ate away at me, there was one tiny crystal of hope. If I could make my peace with the ghost of Hank Williams then I had a chance.

I looked up from my stupor long enough to get a reading on my music, and the bulk of it was shit, plain and simple. I'd been doing the same act for so long that I didn't really give a damn about it one way or the other, and the audience was catching on real fast.

I was writing some good stuff, no doubt. "Stoned at the Jukebox," I had a gut feeling, was a hit. And I was working on some other stuff, too. There was one about Montana, a place in which I'd been hunting for the last few years, and I thought the song was good. I knew that it meant a lot to me. A heck of a lot to me. I also knew what I'd been hearing on the radio was good—southern rock, they called it, and it touched a nerve. I could feel, even through the haze I was living in, that a fusion between that rock and country music was not only possible, it was inevitable. A lot of people had tried to make that kind of music and failed—rejected by either one camp or the other. But I knew I could try and succeed. For once, damn it, I'd make this Williams name work for me instead of against me!

If I could make an album that showed the connection between country and the new rock, then I could look at myself in the mirror in the morning without gagging. I'd be making *my* music, not Daddy's or Mother's or anybody else's.

That was one heck of an idea: my music.

I savored it the way a drunk savors that first taste of whiskey in the morning.

My music.

Music to reach all those kids who didn't go to my concerts anymore. Music for 1974 instead of 1953. A new kind of country music.

I could do it, if I could just live long enough. Which threw me right back into a fit of depression. What good was knowing you had the power if you couldn't live long enough to use it?

But it was a flash of hope, and it was the only flash I had.

Then I found a friend. Gwen and I had seen a psychologist named Dr. Metz, and he'd made more sense than most. We'd even gone hunting together, and I liked him a lot. I was in the hospital in

168

Nashville, for exhaustion or something similar, when I ran into him again. It took him about five seconds to realize what kind of shape I was in, and the next thing I knew he was keeping close tabs on me. One day I finally went to see him, and we had a long talk. He showed me some of the things I'd written while half-delirious in the hospital, like writing my name over and over and over until it became the illegible scrawl of a wild man—which is exactly what it was. He made sense, and we had more talks.

"Number one, Hank: I don't know how you've made it this far in your situation," he told me. "You've always been expected to act like Hank Williams, to be like Hank Williams, to sing like Hank Williams, to look like Hank Williams—the whole thing. I don't really see any other outs. They've almost succeeded. You're almost like Hank Williams—deceased at an early age.

"You've always been a soft touch—oh, Hank'll take care of this, Hank'll take care of that. You've paid a lot of people's incomes out of what you made," Dr. Metz said, and he was right. "I want you to start thinking about yourself and nobody—I mean NOBODY—else. You've never blown any dates; you've been on the road your whole life; you say you owe this to the business, to your mother, to your manager, whatever. I say you owe something to yourself."

It was like hearing the truth for the first time. He said I was trapped in a deadly triangle—"You're watching your mother on one side, whose health is failing and who is a bitter, lonely, depressed woman. Your wife and son are on the other, and that's a total loss. Right? You're fighting with your management. Where does that leave you to turn when you come off the road? You're the odd man out."

So what to do. Yes, what to do?

"Where are your friends, Hank?"

I laughed. Nashville is out, he said, because no matter how hard I try, I'm going to be involved in the music business. Worse, I'm going to be trapped in the myth of Hank Williams.

"Where else, Hank?"

Well, I thought, that's a toughie. There was Granddaddy's place in Alabama, but that wasn't exactly right either.

"Well, I've been fishing with this guy named J. R. Smith, and he lives in Cullman, Alabama," I said. "J. R. and I have gotten to be pretty good friends, and I've been stopping off in Cullman whenever I was down there . . ."

"Great," the doctor said. "If you like the place, great. Because I'm telling you honest—this situation can't go on. You can't take it. I don't care if you have to move to Timbuktu, you've got to get out of Nashville."

That night I called J. R., and the next morning I headed down Interstate 65, south to Alabama.

21

Stoned at the Jukebox

Cullman, Alabama, is about the size of a large living room, three or four thousand people on the good days, and it felt just about as cozy that day in 1975 when I crossed the city limits and headed for J. R. Smith's house. This time, I thought, I'd really done it. I'd left Nashville once and for all. I'd also quit performing, and I didn't give a good damn whether I ever walked back on a stage again.

I'd managed to cause quite a scandal in leaving: "Hank's son leaves Music City; vows to give up business!" I still didn't like reporters.

Everything I owned, which wasn't much, was piled in the back of my blue hotrod truck, and to hell with the rest of it. With my house, my cars, my bands, my wives, my career, my manager, my record company—the golden goose had just flown the coop.

The victory might be a little more complete, a voice in the back of my head rumbled, if the golden goose had managed to bring a little of the gold along with him. I never paid too much attention to money—I'd always had so much of it that the supply seemed like tap water. If I wanted anything badly enough, I could probably afford it. Except those days had just come to a crashing end.

I was broke. I owed everybody for everything, and they were howling like a pack of wolves. My bills, Gwen's bills, Sharon's alimony, road expenses, house and car payments—what I had left was what I had with me, which wasn't much. A little man from the Internal Revenue Service was asking lots of questions around town, and he had a bill that said I owed him $175,000 or thereabouts. Figures that large don't mean anything—it just translates into: "More than I've got." Later, J. R. told me I owed at least $50,000, not counting the money to the Feds.

All I knew, though, driving into Cullman, was that I'd really shown those bastards who was boss, and if I starved to death because of it, well that was just tough luck. Sure, I had no income from performing (which happens to be the bulk of a performer's operating capital). Sure, my royalty money was being eyed by Uncle Sam with a meat cleaver. Sure, my record company contract was running out and they were less than enthused with my antics of the last couple of years. I was sure I'd survive all of it.

When I pulled that truck into the driveway, J. R. Smith was waiting for me, and I felt good inside to have a person like J. R. as my friend.

You might think J. R. Smith is an unreconstructed redneck, and J. R. might even laugh and agree with your evaluation. About that time, if you're smart, you'll start watching your wallet, 'cause J. R. Smith is one shrewd gentleman. He might have an Alabama drawl, but if you underestimate him, he'll have your hide.

He got started in the trucking business at sixteen, and when I pulled into his driveway he was thirty-eight and semiretired. "Semi" meant that he kept an eye on the business; "retired" meant that he usually observed from Panama City, where he kept his fishing boat.

That fishing boat was the reason I came to be involved with J. R.—the boat and Merle Kilgore. Merle had been down in Panama City, roaring, when someone introduced him to J. R. They went

172

fishing, and then they went fishing again, and pretty soon they were fast friends. So fast, in fact, that when Merle began having one of his regular breakups with whichever number wife he was on at the time, he called J. R., and J. R. took him in.

I met J. R. through Merle, and pretty soon the three of us were spending whatever time I could spare in Panama City. Panama City—Lord, I loved to go down there and *roar*! Me and Merle (before Merle settled down, which is another story in itself) would hit those beachside bars like twin hurricanes, going through pills and liquor and those beachside girlies like wind through the pines. I'd get up on those Mickey Mouse stages, borrow some local boy's electric Gibson, and rock and roll until dawn, or until I fell off the stage, whichever came first. Then, the next morning, J. R. would load us up and take us out on his boat, where we could nurse our hangovers to the gentle rocking of the Gulf of Mexico, gracefully staggering to the rail to throw up over the side. Boy, that J. R. sure knew how to have a good time!

We honky-tonked, and sometimes it was good and sometimes it was bad. There's two kinds of honky-tonkin'—one is just for the hell of it, and the other is just to forget. The first, if you don't do it *too* often, just leaves you with a mouthful of cotton and a mind full of resolutions in the morning. It flushes out your system, like sticking a hose in your mouth and leaving it there until the water shoots out of your ears. The second, though, will eat you alive, because what you're looking for is oblivion. That's what I did in Nashville, looking down the necks of bottles. But, sometimes, in Panama City with J. R. and Merle, we touched on the good old hellraising honky-tonkin' I used to know, and, boy, that helped!

J. R. always told me that I should pack it all up and move to Alabama, and he didn't even act surprised when I called him and told him that was exactly what I planned to do. "Well," he said, "ole Merle's moved out and we've got a spare bedroom, so why don't you just move in with us?"

"Us" was J. R., his wife Connie, and their three kids. I was to be Kid Number Four.

Once J. R. got me moved in, the accountant in him couldn't hold back any longer. "Leave it to me," he said, "and I'll see if we can get your finances straightened out." That was fine with me, since whenever I paid attention to them, I managed to screw them up more. The closest I wanted to get to handling my finances was signing checks, something I was genuinely good at. In the meantime I'd just hunt and fish and play my guitar and try to blot the last three years out of my mind. That's what I told everybody, anyway.

How J. R. made heads or tails of my finances, he never explained. I guess it was first convincing everybody that I had nothing, then parceling up that nothing so nobody felt cheated. I needed a business office of some kind, so he set me up in an unused corner of his trucking company. When he tried to have a phone installed, the phone company said, "No dice." They'd checked my records in Nashville, and noticed I had a nasty habit of running up huge bills and then not paying them for months. I'd forgotten that. They'd checked my credit rating, and discovered that if it was possible for a human to have a rating of less than zero, I'd succeeded This was all a nice way of saying I was a bum.

But J. R. wheedled and worked—I had to have a phone in my name, and they finally relented. With J. R. Smith, a citizen in good standing, as cosigner and a paltry deposit of *only* $1,000, they agreed to give me a phone. But the first time the bill was late, *kaput*!

J. R. worked like a dog to build my credit back up. He even tried to sell my truck, since it was the only tangible asset I had. He stopped when he'd discovered that, true to form, I'd paid more for the truck than it was worth, and the price he could get for it wasn't enough to pay off the notes. I got to keep the truck, which I managed to wreck one night on the way to Panama City. Luckily, neither me nor J. R. nor Merle was hurt—the truck only rolled over once.

I appreciated what J. R. was doing: I appreciated the hell out of it. But money wasn't what I had on my mind. For the most part, neither was my career.

174

What occupied my mind was Gwen. I had moved the body to Alabama, but the soul was still rooted in Tennessee. All that mattered was getting her back, now that I'd so obviously lost her. I was on the phone constantly, talking to her, pleading with her, trying to find some common ground where we could start building again. I even managed to talk her into coming to Alabama once in a very rare while, although we were hardly man and wife when she was there.

Once we'd gone to a dinner party, myself and Gwen, J. R. and Connie, at some club, and the man giving the party recognized me and talked me into getting up on stage. I didn't particularly want to, but I couldn't see any polite way out of it. As I went on stage, he told me he wanted to hear some of that great music my daddy did. Oh boy. So I started into one of Daddy's songs, "I'm So Lonesome I Could Cry," I think, and I was doing a perfect imitation until I just thought, "What the hell?" So I jazzed it up a little, sped up the tempo, and changed the phrasing. It sounded like a different song.

Gwen got up from the table and came toward the stage. "Well," I said, "it looks like my wife here has a request." Then I covered the microphone with my hand.

"Play the song right!" she hissed. "These people don't want to hear *you!*" Then she sat back down.

"She just wants to hear another one of Daddy's songs," I told the audience, and boiling inside, I did another one. Then I sat back down. Visits were always pleasant, just like that.

After almost a year, I moved out of J. R.'s spare bedroom into an A-frame cabin on the city reservoir. It was beautiful, so far out in the country that people would really have to look to find me. The A-frame was small and cozy, with just room enough for one person to knock around. I could have target practice out my back door, with hunting and fishing within easy walking distance. It was everything Nashville wasn't, and I still couldn't shake the depression that wrapped around my mind like a snake. Like Daddy said, the blues come around at midnight. They were like animals, hiding in the nooks and crannies of my new house, just waiting until I climbed the steps to the bedroom to creep up behind me and pounce. I knew what I was doing was right. I knew, like Dr. Metz said, that this was the only thing that could preserve my sanity and my life. But just about the time I'd reach out to shut off the light, I'd see them, hiding behind a door or under the bed, just biding their time.

Sure enough, I'd close my eyes and they'd attack, and the whole grim routine would start unfolding in front of my eyes. I'd live every mistake again and again. Say every stupid thing a million times. Go from the top of the world to the bottom in one easy step. I'd see my successes turn into failures, see people laughing at me behind my back. I'd imagine my son being forced into the music business, just like I was, and I'd feel so sick inside. Every night.

Sometimes I'd get up and call Gwen, which would never end in any satisfactory manner. Sometimes I'd call J. R. or Merle and cry while they'd listen. And sometimes I'd just hop in whatever car or truck was available and going tearing along the country backroads until I'd spent the worst of it. Then I'd go home, take a bunch of sleeping pills, and go to sleep.

Sometimes those sleeping pills seemed like the only answer. "Take us," they seemed to say. "You've managed to screw up everything else. So why not just take us and get this whole thing over with? Why not?"

One night I did. It wasn't a night any different from those I'd been having for the last three years. Maybe that was the problem. Maybe I was just sick and tired of having nights like that. Maybe I just couldn't bring myself to face another one tomorrow.

So I took a bottle of Darvon, just turned it up and emptied it like a shot of Jim Beam. No clever notes. A quick goodbye call to Gwen. No cryptic messages for the heirs. I was just ready to die.

Then again, maybe I hadn't totally forgotten that the local handyman was scheduled to stop over later to do some work on the place. Maybe I was hedging my bet. Maybe I wasn't.

But he found me and called J. R., who raced over and started walking me around. Then he loaded me in the car and took me to a local doctor—I refused to go to Nashville. They pumped my stomach and fed me coffee until *that* was enough to kill me, and the next day I didn't try again. I just sort of filed it under Future Operations. "Next time," I thought wryly, "I'll be more thorough." Leave it to me to screw up my own suicide.

Gwen flew down in the morning, but she left by midafternoon. We didn't have much to say to each other, and it dawned on me when she left that it was all over except for the crying and the court and how big a piece of me she wanted to carve out and keep. "Welcome to 1975," I thought. "It's going to be one hell of a year."

The only thing I had left to me was my music, and I finally threw myself into the idea I'd been nurturing in my head for so long. I wanted to do a special album of my own music, done my own way. It would be totally different from anything I'd ever done before, and I knew I was taking a hell of a risk—I'd even had hit songs in 1974. "Last Love Song" was a number one song. If I walked away from that, there was a chance I'd never get it back.

Still, I was totally determined. For one thing, I refused to record in Nashville again. I wanted no part of *that* scene. Instead, we'd go to Muscle Shoals, Alabama, where the studios have a decided funkier, rhythm-and-blues feel about them. Instead of the same old Nashville pickers who'd worked on every one of my albums since Day One, I'd use southern rock people.

That's what I'd do—the best of the new. It'd be different, and, more importantly, it'd be me. And it was a straw to hang on to in the hurricane in my mind.

22

"Friends"

While my Nashville lawyers worked to straighten out my personal life, I concentrated—for the first time in a long while—on my music. For a start, I began talking to Phil Walden, the president of Capricorn Records, in Macon, Georgia, and the man who'd launched the Allman Brothers and the Marshall Tucker Band. Phil was sort of the godfather of southern rock and roll, as well as the fellow who'd help launch Otis Redding, one of the greatest R & B singers of our time, and I was sure he'd be open to what I had in mind. He was, and he arranged the introductions between me and the Brothers and the Tuckers. Toy Caldwell of the Marshall Tucker Band and I got pretty close—the band had been tossed out of gigs in South Carolina for playing Hank Williams' songs, and he'd been a fan of mine as long as I'd been a fan of his.

So I just mentioned, off the top of my head-like, that I was getting ready to do another album, and I wondered if any of you Macon boys might want to do a little pickin'. The response was totally overwhelming.

"Hell, yea," they said. "Son, we've *always* been ready, willing, and able to play country music. We was just waiting for someone to ask.''

''Before you start practicing those Hank Williams songs,'' I cautioned them, ''wait a bit. This album is going to be something special; it ain't gonna be *old* Hank, it's gonna be *new* Hank.'' When I played them a couple of my songs, they whistled. This album *was* going to be something special.

I'd been squirreling away some of my best songs until something like this record came along. I had my song about Montana, and that was one of my absolute favorites, ever. I'd also written my last love song for Gwen, called ''I Really Did'': ''I loved you, I really did . . .'' There was a song about a girl in Clovis, New Mexico, and one I'd just thrown off the top of my head, ''Brothers of the Road'':

> You got fortune and fame and a well-known name
> And you're really riding high.
> Whether you're rock or country, blues or funky
> We're all the same inside.
> Living in fear of the later years
> When nobody's gonna want us around
> You know, brothers of the road
> All share the same load,
> And it'll just about bring you down.
> if you let it, it'll bring you down . . .

But the enthusiasm of that song belied the lyrics—sure, it might bring you down, but if you keep on pickin', you'll be all right. That song cooked!

I'd also decided to cut two of Toy's songs that had become standards for the Marshall Tucker Band—''Can't You See'' and ''Losin' You.'' Nobody in Nashville had looked to Macon for material, and I practically quivered when I thought about it. I'd been in the business awhile, long enough to know that those two songs were stone country hits. And rock hits, if they were handled correctly. FM radio was just coming into its own—album rock, they called it, and the deejays were already heavy into West Coast "country-rock" acts like the Eagles and Linda Ronstadt and even old Gram Parsons and the Flying Burrito Brothers material. That's not to mention such stuff as the Allman Brothers' "Ramblin Man," which to my ears was a country song. I knew that the artificial barriers between the music couldn't last for much longer—they just couldn't! Kids aren't that dumb. One day they're going to turn on the radio and realize that it was time to change the dial and find some of the originals. I knew the kids were going to come looking for country music, and I intended to be there.

Cutting "Can't You See" and "Losin' You" was like walking through the woods and stumbling over two diamonds. They couldn't miss!

I also added "Stoned at the Jukebox" and a beautiful ballad written by one of Nashville's great unsung talents, Vince Matthews, called "On Susan's Floor." The song had been cut before by Gordon Lightfoot, but the first time I'd heard it, I knew it was meant for me.

The album needed one last song, and I knew what it was going to be. It was going to be the most important song I'd ever written. It was going to be the exclamation point at the end of the old Hank Williams Junior. I'd been working on it for some time, and I called it "Living Proof":

> I'm gonna quit singing all them sad songs
> 'Cause I can't stand the pain
> For the life I sing to you about
> And the one I live is the same
>
> When I sing them old songs of Daddy's
> Seems like every one comes true
> Lord, please help me
> Do I have to be
> The Living Proof?

It almost tore me up inside to write it. Just like "Standing in the

Shadows" so long ago, this was my life. Every word was the stone
cold truth, and it hurt. Lord, how it hurt!

> Just the other night after a show
> An old drunk came up to me
> He said "You ain't as good as your daddy, boy,
> And you never will be."
>
> Then a young girl in old blue jeans.
> Said "I'm your biggest fan."
> It's a good thing I
> Was born Gemini
> 'Cause I'm living for more than one man.
>
> Remember Jimmie and Hank and Johnny
> They were in the summer of life
> When you called them away, Lord
> I don't want to pay that price.
>
> Don't let my son ever touch a guitar
> May he never sing the blues
> Let him be free
> Don't make him be
> More Living Proof.

In a lot of ways it was a prayer. "Living Proof" was a song I had
to write because it helped me put my life into focus, and I needed
that more than I needed anything else in the world.

> I don't want to be a legend
> I just want to be a man
> And Lord, you know sometimes
> I've needed a helping hand
> And it ain't been so easy lately.
> I've had to go it all alone
> But I've always had everything I've ever wanted
> Except a home.
>
> I'm gonna quit singing all these sad songs.
> 'Cause I can't stand the pain

An Autobiography

For the life I sing about, Lord,
And the one I live is the same.
Yes I've sang them old songs of daddy's
And it seems they've all come true
Lord, please help me.
Do I have to be
The Living Proof?

Catharsis.

I felt better than I'd felt in years when I finished writing that song. Sure, the demons were all still there; I could just catch a glimpse of them behind a door or under the bed. But I think I had them controlled. I could get up in the morning and stand to face the next day.

I called Music Mill Studios in Muscle Shoals and booked studio time for February, to record an album tentatively titled "Hank Williams Junior and Friends."

I'd been duck hunting in Paris, Tennessee, when time came to go into the studio, and since I'm a hopeless procrastinator when it comes to leaving a hunting trip, my friend Bill Dyer agreed to fly me from Paris to Muscle Shoals in his plane. As usual, I got there in the nick of time. All the sessions' men were already there, in their cowboy hats and flashy cowboy shirts. I went straight in wearing my camouflage outfit and waist-high rubber waders.

"Hi," I said to a lot of puzzled looks. "I'm Hank, and let's make some music."

And boy, did we ever! Into the spring and right on into summer, we worked. I was joined by Toy Caldwell and Dickie Betts and Chuck Leavell—Chuck and Dickie were from the Allman Brothers—with Charlie Daniels joining in on tape, and I worked like I'd never worked before. Dickie had to leave early—women troubles, and I sympathized—but the rest of us slammed away.

We finished in July, and the album was everything I hoped it would be. It was my masterpiece, and I had a gut feeling that it was the right album at the right time. I went to the Capricorn Records

183

picnic as soon as I finished, and it felt great. Everybody who had worked on the album had talked about it, and the air was electric with anticipation. It felt great!

I'd even decided to try going back on the road, although that scared me shitless. I knew what the road had done to me, and despite all my braggadocio, I was still treading a narrow knife's-edge. I was under control, but only by the barest margin. I hadn't been able to shake the drugs or liquor, the blues still came around at midnight, and I had to almost physically restrain myself to keep from making a late-night call to Nashville and Gwen.

True to form, when the album was finished and the picnic was over and I was left to my own devices, I felt those old demons creeping back.

Damn it!

I resolved to keep myself extremely busy until it was time to go back on the road.

I decided to learn to fly. Which was perfect, since it was time-consuming and complicated, as well as something I really wanted to learn how to do. I wholeheartedly threw myself into flying, all through the waning weeks of July. I took lessons in Panama City, and even J. R. was amazed at my progress. In less than a month I had my license.

It was almost August 1975, and I planned to go back on the road in September, for better or for worse. The only other thing I had planned for the autumn was a sheep hunt in Canada, and boy, that was going to be an experience! Just what I needed. The more I thought about it, the more I realized how out of shape I'd become and there was no way I could face that ordeal in the shape I was in.

So I started working out, lifting weights and jogging, trying to shake off three or four years of abuse. Just to be sure I'd be in shape, I called my friend Dick Willey in Montana. "How'd you like for me to come out and do some hiking and climbing for a while?" I asked. "Just to get in shape."

"The heck, Hank," Dick said—he always said "the heck," or sometimes "the hell"—"we'd love to have you!"

184

It sounded good, and I figured it might help me get myself ready for the road. The more I thought about it, in fact, the more I knew I *had* to go, and I made my plans for the first week of August 1975.

· Then I went to Nashville, not to play at the music business, but to look at airplanes. I had this real urge to buy an airplane—God knows how I planned to pay for it, although J. R., over the last year, had renegotiated this last album with MGM, beaten the wolves away from the door, and managed to get me in pretty good shape financially. To make a long story short, I bought a plane, and I was looking at some others a little while later when the dealer, an old friend named C. F. Lautner, had a unique idea.

"Hank," he said, "I'm going to fix you up with a girl."

Great. Just what I needed. I wandered around his office, picking up this and that, looking out the window at the planes.

"I've got just the right girl in mind . . ."

I walked over to his desk and picked up a picture lying there. It was of a softball team, and there was one girl who stood out like a diamond.

"How about this girl?" I said, pointing to the girl in the picture.

"You wouldn't like her," he said. "Now, the one I've got in mind . . ."

"No, I want to know about this girl." I was adamant. "What's her name? Where does she work? Is she married? Do you think she could love a country singer?" I was definitely getting carried away.

"Aw, Hank. Her name is Becky and she works at ABC Records, and I suppose you want a date with her."

Absolutely, I said. "The other girl I've got in mind is much better," he said. "I mean, she's . . . well . . . you know . . . *wilder.*" "No dice," I said. "The one in the picture or nothing."

Grumbling, he dialed the number. "Becky? Campbell Lauther here. Are you doing anything tonight?" He paused. "Well, you are now." He reached across and handed me the phone.

Think fast, hoss!

"Hello, Becky? Hi, this is Hank Williams Junior, and you don't

185

know me, but I just bought an airplane and I'm broke. Could you take me out to dinner tonight?''

Long silence.

''Hello?''

''Weeeelllll . . .''

What a drawl! That girl had a southern drawl that just wouldn't quit!

''Weeellll, who did you say this was?''

''Hank Williams Junior.''

Long silence.

''Weeellll, I guess it'd be all right, just for supper.'' Actually what she *really* said was ''Weeeellll, ah guess it'd be aw-write for suh-pper.''

''Pick you up at seven, then?''

''Weeeellll, okay.''

We exchanged addresses, and when I hung up I could almost shout with joy! It's a little hard to explain why I was so excited, unless maybe you want to attribute some of it to Fate. All I knew was that I had a feeling this was going to be *good*, and I needed that. I could hardly wait until evening!

What Becky did when I hung up was to ask her friend Charlotte Tucker, who worked with her at ABC, if (1) she'd ever heard of somebody named Hank Williams Junior, since Becky hadn't, and (2) if that person was known to be a maniac, sex or otherwise. Charlotte gave her a mixed report—that he was a big star and that there were ''stories'' about him. That he sang real good, and that what could you lose from a dinner date? And call as soon as you get in!

So we went to dinner, a cozy affair with me and Becky, Merle, and Bill Dyer, my hunting buddy, and his wife, Betty. I didn't want Becky to feel uncomfortable, first date and all. It was wonderful, all I could have hoped for. She was wonderful! Then we all went and saw *Jaws*. That was pretty good, too.

When I took her home that evening, I stayed around and talked for a long time, and I guess I talked like I hadn't talked to anyone in years. She talked, too. She was an ex-stewardess, and I'd caught her at the end of her own longterm love affair. She'd been hurt, and hurt badly, but my phone call was just too much to resist. We talked for hours, and then I kissed her goodnight and left.

At the risk of sounding just a little bit silly, I left walking on clouds. I'd had experience with a lot of things, but love at first sight wasn't one of them. Until now. Lust at first sight was a different story.

I saw her the next day, and the next, and the next, and the next, and mostly we talked. She was scared of relationships, and I was battered, and we fit together like, as she would say in her Louisiana drawl, two peas in a pod. I told her I was thinking ahead, to a time when I wouldn't be singing, when I was forty-five or fifty years old. What would I be doing then? Whom would I be with then? I could almost feel her recoil, and I thought, "You damn fool, you've scared her off!" But she stuck.

It seems like we spent a lifetime there in Nashville, just sitting and talking, but it was only one week. One week and I could already feel just the tiniest bit of healing touch my soul. I was in love with this woman. But was it enough?

We were back at my motel, finishing off the evening with more talking and, well, maybe a bit of kissing and hugging. Tomorrow I'd be leaving for Montana—I'd been trying hard enough. The airlines were on strike. All the flights out of Nashville were booked solid. It was so frustrating I could have screamed!

"I'll tell you, Hank," J. R. said a couple of days earlier. "Maybe somebody's telling you you ought to stay in Nashville and not go out there."

I snorted in disgust and finally got a flight that took about a year to get to Billings. Another year to get to Missoula.

"Maybe I'm not supposed to go to Montana," I told Becky. "Maybe I'm supposed to stay here and be with you."

Maybe I wanted her to beg me to stay, too. Maybe I wanted to hear her say, "Stay. I love you." But her daddy was a hunter, and she'd learned on her daddy's knee that one thing you don't *ever* do is try to talk a man out of going hunting. She was silent, and we kissed again. Then I looked into her eyes and took a deep breath:

"I love you," I said, and I meant it more than I'd ever meant anything in my life.

She looked startled and scared all at the same time, and then she looked back into my eyes.

"Well," she said, "I like you a lot, Hank. Maybe I love you too. But I don't want to get tied down right now. I don't know. I just don't know."

"We need time to think," I told her between kisses. "I need time to think about a lot of things. We can talk when I get back."

She laughed a little and then she left, and I felt the blues seeping in beneath the door as she closed it. I loved her, but I was so scared!

I picked up the phone and called the bellhop.

"Send me up a fifth of Jim Beam. And a broad, if you can find one." A few minutes later there was a knock on the door.

The next morning, hung over and more than a little ashamed, I got on an airplane bound for Montana, to keep an appointment on the side of old Ajax.

23

Once and for All

Pause, while my life divides neatly into two parts, with a line right down the middle from a mountaintop in Montana stretching out toward infinity. Sometimes I wake up at night thinking about it, how easily the Lord can wipe His hand across your life and leave nothing the same. Especially inside your head.

The first show after the fall was anticlimactic. It was in Delaware, and it took place in May of 1976, nine months after that afternoon on the side of old Ajax. In a lot of ways it was as if I'd never been away—the stage was the same; the lights were the same; the band was the same. I was the only part that was different.

Funny. My old friends would drop by and spend some time, and they'd leave scratching their heads. "You're not the same guy," they'd say. "The body's sure as hell not the same, and neither is the person in it." And boy, that made me feel so good!

The hardest part of the show was just lasting through the whole set—I was still weak, weaker than I'd even let myself believe. But I could still sing, and I could play the guitar one heck of a lot better than before, and, damn it all, I was good!

I played my music. Not Daddy's music. Not Mother's music. But my own music. That's not saying I didn't play some of Daddy's songs, because that would be lying. They're *still* some of the greatest songs ever written. But ole Hank's reincarnation had finally hung up his guitar, and Hank Williams Junior had a story to tell.

To be honest, the crowd wasn't what I'd seen in the past. That was a fact I was prepared to face, now. I might never see the kinds of crowds I'd seen before, and I might never be the biggest star in country music ever again.

What I could do was walk out on that stage and sing, and, Lord, I savored the experience! To say I was singing prayers of thanks wouldn't be far from right. I was my own man, and I wasn't afraid of looking into corners anymore. For the first time in years, I looked out at that audience and all I saw was friends. Not worthless bastards looking for a piece of Hank Williams Junior. Not people trying to rip me off or stuff me in a particular pigeonhole. Just people, people who wanted to hear me play the guitar and sing. "What do you think of that, Daddy?" I thought, accepting my applause. "Your Bocephus is a survivor."

I'd made another important decision, too—one that was to have an incredibly large impact on my life, to say the least.

I'd decided I wasn't going to be a hermit. In any sense of the word.

Actually, the decision was pretty much out of my hands, thanks to a case of feminine wiles. But I'd better begin at the beginning of the story.

While Becky White was sitting around Nashville thinking about the madman she'd met the week before, the one who'd said he was in love with her and then run away to Montana, she got a call from Charlotte Tucker.

"Have you heard?" Charlotte told her. "Hank fell off a mountain, and he's hurt real bad!"

She hadn't heard, and that wasn't the best way to hear anything.

190

A whole series of frantic phone calls followed, and luckily, Dick Willey finally got back to her. Her first inclination was, of course, to catch the first plane out.

"Don't," Dick advised. "There's nothing you can do here, and his whole family is already on the way. It'd be better for both you and Hank if you stayed in Nashville for a while."

Dick did his best to keep her up to date. But Dick also had other ideas. Gwen was already there, by my bedside, and Dick wasn't sure just exactly how much of the outside world I was perceiving. All Dick knew was that Gwen was pledging her undying love again, and Dick knew where that road led.

"This is a circus out there," Dick said to Becky. "You don't want to be caught up in it. But you've got to call him. You've got to write him. It's important that he knows you're there."

As soon as I could take calls, I was getting them from Becky, and letters as well. When I found out the truth about my face, when I made my resolves, I tried to let her down as gently as I could. If she could see me, she'd understand. But I didn't want her to see me. I didn't want that at all!

She kept on calling anyway.

Dick used to joke about her accent when she'd call his house while I was convalescing there.

"Hannnnnnnnnk!," he'd drawl in the very worst imitation of a southern drawl I'd ever heard. "Hannnnnnnnnk! It's Beckkkkkkkkkkkkeeeeeee!" All the while encouraging her calls. "Forget what he says," he'd tell her. "You ought to see how his eyes light up whenever you call. You just keep calling, girl!"

The harder I tried to let her go, the tougher she hung on. We talked about trivia—who was doing what to whom in Music City, what she was doing with her time, the new guitar–gun–hat I'd bought in Montana. It was a little island of the way the world used to be.

But I was resolved, and I can be a stubborn cuss. I was a monster, and I'd foist myself off on no woman, much less one that I loved. (There, it kept coming back to haunt me, night after night, I'd met the girl of my dreams, and was being forced to give her up. Of it all, that was the hardest to accept.)

When I got back to Alabama, she wanted to see me.

It took all my strength, and it was still just about the hardest thing I ever had to do.

"No," I told the woman I loved. "I don't ever want to see you again. Please understand me. Please."

She agreed, more or less.

I made regular trips to Nashville for physical therapy, usually in the home of an old friend of mine (and Becky's), a woman named Christine Longyear.

One afternoon I was resting after a tough session when Christine came back to talk to me. She looked very sheepish.

"Becky's here, and she wants to see you," Christine said.

I was furious, and I'd have been even more furious if I'd known that Christine had been plotting this for weeks. She wanted to be sure I was in no position to just walk away without seeing Becky.

"Well, I don't want to see her."

"She says she won't leave until she talks to you, Hank, and I think she means it." Christine was practically shoving me through the door into the room where Becky was.

"All right, but only for a second, Christine." I was steaming when she led me into the room, and there she was, more beautiful than I'd even remembered.

"Hi," I said. I was *so* conscious of the way I looked. Of the hole in my forehead and the scars all over my face and my eye that wouldn't focus. I was still a monster—at least, to me I was.

"Hello, Hank."

"I thought I told you that I didn't want to see you again."

"You did. But, oh, Hank, I wanted to see you! I've worked so hard! I've been letting my fingernails grow. I've lost a lot of weight. And I want you to see me. I've done all this for you!"

Women! She sort of turned on one heel while my whole carefully constructed world fell apart. What rushed in to fill the void was love. My eyes just couldn't see enough of her! And she was smiling, so happy-like. I searched her eyes for some trace of revulsion and there just wasn't any there. "You were always still Hank," she told me later. "To tell you the truth, I don't even think I really noticed what you looked like."

I don't think she did, either.

The next week, she came to Cullman to help me out in the cabin. The first night she slept in the spare bedroom. The next day was beautiful, and we walked in the woods and talked. Then we made love, for the very first time, and she stayed in my room that night. I knew then I never wanted her to leave.

That was in March, before the operation on my forehead. We were never apart very much after that, although I feared what would happen to her when the divorce proceedings with Gwen actually came down. I should never have worried. When the time did come, Becky was a tower of strength. No groveling under an attorney's insinuating questions. She just went in, said she loved me and that we were lovers, and that was that. Shot the hell out of the case, which was predicated on proving that I was "living in sin" with another woman. Still cost me a fortune, though.

While that decision filled me with joy, something else was filling me with dread. MGM was getting ready to release "Hank Williams Junior and Friends," and I was scared. Scared on two fronts. I knew what the album represented. How would the public accept it? How would they react to a "new" Hank Williams Junior? And in the strictly nuts-and-bolts sense, MGM was never very good with albums.

The main problem was that they clung like lint to the old ways of doing business, and one of those ways was to emphasize the single over the album. The definition of an album was one hit single with nine filler cuts, and that was generally true of country music. Rock and roll had realized a long time back that there was no future in going for one hit single: There were so many advantages to albums that the choice was terribly simple. For one thing—and this was something dear to every artist's and record producer's heart—albums made lots more money.

For another thing, the sound on an album is about 1,000 times better, which is good for both the artist and the listener. Also, an album gives an artist—if he does it right—a much broader palette to work on. "Hank Williams Junior and Friends," in that sense, was much more like a rock album than a country one. The album as a whole made a statement; there was no filler material anywhere.

But MGM still lived in the good ole days. The fact that I'd produced one hell of an album didn't leave much of an effect on their corporate mentality.

No matter how hard I tried, I couldn't get them to see beyond the single. How this all came up was in the process of picking a single release from the album. The regional promotion men—the guys who go around to every radio station in the country and explain to the deejays why they should be playing such-and-such a record—were very enthusiastic. "Release any one of those cuts," they told their bosses. "This stuff is the perfect music at the perfect time. Country music is getting ready to rock and roll a little, and this could be *dynamite*!" (Promotion men really talk that way, by the way. Dynamite.)

Go with "Stoned at the Jukebox" or even "Brothers of the Road." Better yet, go with one of the Toy Caldwell numbers—they could be the sleepers. I wanted either "Can't You See" or "Losin' You," because both those songs were single hits, and both would bring you back to the album: "*This* is Hank Williams Junior? Well, maybe we'd better take another look!" I wanted people to come back to the album. Damn it, that was the important thing!

MGM released the album in their monthly package, with thirty-two other releases. No fanfare, no promotion, nothing.

Still they stalled about the single. That single was very important to country radio stations, because, as a rule, a country jock won't play a cut off an album. They'll hold off for the single.

FM progressive rock stations picked up the album, and the cut

194

they played the most often was "Can't You See." It was a first—a hard country artist like me making *any* inroads into that FM market.

The reviews began to come back—raves. All raves! From *Rolling Stone* which routinely refused to review country albums except as novelty items. From *The Village Voice* in New York City, another paper distinctly cool to anything that even hinted of country music: "one of the ten best albums of the year!" A lot of people have talked about fusing country and blues and rock and rhythm-and-blues, the *Voice* said. Now the son of Hank Williams has done it!

MGM called me in Alabama and told me they were going to release "Living Proof" as the single.

"NO!" I shouted. "You can't!" When I calmed down, I did my best to explain. "Living Proof" may well be a great song, but it had to be seen in the context of the album as a whole. It was the *one* song on the album that *couldn't* be plucked out there for a single. It was vitally important that you hear the whole album *before* "Living Proof" to really understand who Hank Junior was and what he was trying to do! Otherwise, there's one hell of a danger of the whole thing backfiring, and me getting written off as somebody still trying to ride his daddy's coattails. Please, I asked them, go with "Can't You See."

MGM was adamant. They explained how much money they'd made (for me as well as for them) by making sure everyone knew whose son I was. And, yes, all this other music was interesting, but they preferred to go with a sure thing. Yes, it was nice that those rock stations were playing my record, but, after all, it was all those country listeners who really mattered. People who had listened to my daddy.

At least think it over, I begged.

They did, for a day. I'd been at my grandfather's in Alabama when they called back. They'd thought about it, and they were going with "Living Proof."

195

"Then you can Goddamned well shove 'Living Proof,' up your ass!" I shouted into the phone, "Because that's the last release of Hank Williams Junior that MGM Records is ever going to have!"

That wasn't quite true. They released one more album that they had in the can. "Living Proof," wasn't a hit—it made the top thirteen. In fact, just as I'd predicted, a number of disc jockies grumbled about riding Daddy's coattails one time too many.

I was playing a show in Louisana with Waylon Jennings, whose career was getting ready to take off in a big way. Before the show we were sitting around talking.

"Tell me, hoss," he said. He calls everybody hoss. "You're not going to release 'Can't You See'?"

I can't, I told him, and gave him the whole story.

"But, hoss, that song's a hit!"

"I know that, but what can I do? MGM has the right to pick the singles. It's in the contract."

"Well, if you're not going to release it, *I* sure as hell am!" Waylon said, and I told him to do it with my blessing. The next week he was in the studio in Nashville, cutting "Can't You See."

Waylon released it as soon as he could, and it was a huge hit. A hit that changed a lot of people's minds about what country music was all about.

In the middle of it all, Mother died.

She died a broken, bitter woman. Before she died she'd opened our house to tourists, and sold off Hank Williams' memorabilia. She accused J. R. of stealing me away from her. I wish it hadn't ended that way, Lord! I wish.

She was buried in Montgomery, next to Daddy, and it was one of the first times I'd made a big public appearance. One report said I looked like Death itself. Flamboyant New Orleans preacher Bob Harrington delivered the eulogy, then he sang a chorus of "Hey, Good Lookin'." Then he posed for pictures praying over my daddy's grave.

"Please, Lord," I prayed. "I know I've been spared for something. But You're going to have to give me strength. . . ." I

196

watched the people of Montgomery, black and white, file by while the long black limo pulled away. "There are two legends here now," I thought. "Hank and Miss Audrey."

The limo made its stately progress, and if you listened close enough, you could hear the trains clanking in the railroad yard next door.

I survived.

24

The New South

I survived, but to what end?

Regardless of our relationship in the last years of her life, Mother's death shook me badly. For one thing, I was forced to once again face the demons that had almost killed me so many times before.

People whispered. They talked about the Williams Curse, and that poor boy, so much like his daddy. I hurt, but the hurt didn't seem to be part of a universal conspiracy to drive me to an early grave. For the first time I saw rumors for what they really are: words, and nothing more. Hurt was something you could live with.

But again, to what end?

How many angels can dance on the head of a pin, while you're at it? The question still dogged my mind, though, no matter how rhetorical it might be. I was spared from certain death, and I couldn't help but believe there was a price attached to that.

Part of that price I already knew—I would never, *could* never, go back to being the person I once was. That person *did* die on the side of old Ajax; of that I was sure. The only thing I could do was to continue trying to integrate what I had learned into my everyday life; I didn't know what else to do except take one step at a time.

The failure of "Hank Williams Junior and Friends" was another stone in my heart. I knew I could sing. I knew I could perform. But I didn't know whether I'd ever make another album as good as "Friends." I knew I had to come back with another album very soon for my own piece of mind—I'd fallen off the horse, and it was time to get up and start riding again.

Amazingly enough, J.R. had managed to wrangle me a deal with Warner Brothers Records even before he knew whether I'd be able to sing or not! Nice trick, and nobody was sure exactly how that came about. As far as J. R.'ll go is to say that they must have "wanted Hank Junior pretty bad." It didn't hurt that Mike Curb, the president of MGM Records at its heyday and my producer on several records, had an independent deal with Warner and pushed *hard*.

Warner Brothers looked like a very good deal for me. Warner was mainly a pop label, which meant that we could dispense immediately with, for lack of a better word, all the bull that seems to hold country record labels back. Warner Brothers understood about albums. The company wanted to make some inroads into the country market, and they were trying to build up a heavyweight country stable, and I was going to be part of that stable. Assuming, of course, I could still sing.

As soon as we could swing it—right after I'd gone back on stage in May, as a matter of fact—I headed for the studio in Muscle Shoals to do some work. The result was an album called "One Night Stands," and I can't say that it was my best work.

It was really a test run, to see how I'd fit back in the studio after such an absence. In that sense, it was okay. As every critic from here to there pointed out, though, it wasn't "Friends." I'd expected that, but it still stung.

There weren't a lot of my own songs on there, either. There were two. I hadn't exactly been in the mood for songwriting lately. There was a real good rocking version of Merle Kilgore's "I'm Not

Responsible" that I'm still using in my stage shows, so it wasn't all bad.

"The New South" was another story altogether. That was the next album, and you'd better believe I worked hard on that one! I wanted to show Warner that they hadn't made a mistake when they signed me up, and I wanted to show my fans—what fans I still had left—that I was getting ready to come out of the woods, and come out rocking.

I worked with Waylon as my producer, which in a way was kind of strange. We'd become very close friends recently, although it seemed like we'd known each other forever. Like when I was about fourteen and was touring with my mother's Caravan of Stars. I used to sneak over to Waylon's bus and beg the guys to let me drive that old thing, and once I drove it right off the side of the road and knocked all the hubcaps off. Waylon and I used to drag those old posters out and have a good laugh. "See," I'd tell him. "I carried you for a while; now it's your turn to carry me."

Waylon would turn all serious-like. He'd become, while I was lounging around in this hospital, one of the biggest stars country music had ever produced, and it was weighing pretty heavy on his shoulders. Waylon couldn't walk out on the street without drawing a crowd, and I understood how isolated that could make a person. That was one of the things that bound us together.

"Shit, hoss," Waylon would say to me. "You know this don't last for anybody. I'll burn out, and then you'll have to haul me around for a couple of years again."

So we were working together on "The New South," and it felt good. We spent a lot of time discussing each move we made; Waylon was hardly the autocrat. I was able to keep my own input going strong, while at the same time have a second opinion that I could really trust.

We wanted to try a few different things, some of which worked better than others, I might add with a little hindsight. We did bluegrass, with Bill Monroe's "Uncle Pen," and we did good old hard-drinking country music, Vic McAlpin's "How's My Ex Treating

201

You." We recorded two songs from Steve Young, another really great underrated songwriter who'd written, a long time ago, a song called "Seven Bridges Road." Steve Young and I are, in an odd way, soul brothers. He shares my obsession—and I'm afraid that's the only word for it—with Daddy, and in many ways he can see clearer than I can. Plus, he writes great songs.

We also recorded one of Daddy's, but if you didn't know it, you'd never recognize it: "You're Gonna Change (Or I'm Gonna Leave)," done the way I've always wanted to do it, as a blues number. I think that's the way Daddy would be doing it now, if he was still around.

I'd also managed to start writing again, because I found songwriting to be a great way to express the changes I'd gone (and was still going) through. "Feelin Better" said it all, just right there in the title:

> I'm feelin' better;
> I got hurt, but I'm back on the road,
> Gettin' it together
> Between Macon and Muscle Shoals
>
> It all came together
> In my sweet Alabama home
> And I'm through forever
> Tryin' to put everybody on . . .

My songwriting was becoming, if that's possible, even more personal. It was vitally important to me to explain to the public how I'd changed. I wrote three songs for "The New South," and they were all, to one extent or the other, about the new Hank Williams Junior.

There was one song especially that meant an awful lot to me, and that was one I'd written for Becky. It was called "Once and for All," and we recorded it with just me, a guitar, and Waylon's harmony:

Time is catching up with me
  'Cause I've been on the road
And the keys to the city
  Are all I've got to show
Though it's easy to take home
  The belle of the ball
I'm getting tired of it all

And I'm gonna love you
  Once and for all.

'Cause you're the one
  Who stuck it out
And you know that's what love
  Is all about.
I could have a woman every time I called
But I'd rather see you
  Walking down the hall
'Cause I'm gonna love you
  Once and for all
Until the final curtain falls . . .

Taking chances, I guess, is what it's all about, from the music business right down to doing your grocery shopping. "The New South" was a chance, and it was a good album. It didn't take off and make me a superstar overnight, again. You can hash over the reasons for that until you're blue in the face, but what it comes down to is that there really isn't a reason, except that change takes time. And it's scary, I've got to do what I've got to do. And I know that in the end I'll find that audience that appreciates just me. I'm prepared to wait.

Of course, that doesn't mean I don't get mad—as mad as hell sometimes. Dr. Metz told me that I needed to be a mean son-of-a-bitch to survive, and I haven't forgotten that for one minute. Now I know which direction I'm going in, and mean sons-of-bitches seem to have a better chance of arriving intact.

Oh, Becky White and I were married June 18, 1976, at a little church in her hometown of Mer Rouge, Louisiana. Not a lot of people from Nashville were there at the wedding—Waylon and his wife, Jessi Colter, of course; Merle, who wouldn't miss a friend's wedding for the world; Jerry Rivers, from mine and Daddy's old band. It was beautiful.

There was never any doubt in my mind, not since she forced herself on me during my therapy session. "Hank," this voice kept telling me, "if it's like this during the bad times, think of how it's going to be in the good!" For once, I listened to that voice very carefully.

Taking chances, that's what it's all about.

25

Montana Song (Reprise)

There are those who believe that any event, no matter how insignificant, is somehow repeated endlessly, trapped in a tiny portion of time like a prehistoric dragonfly trapped in amber. For want of a better word, we talk about the spirit of a place, or of the spirits who inhabit a place.

The spirits of the mountains are like the gentlest brush of wind against your cheek, because man's hand has lain very lightly on these mountains, and the spirit words are content to whisper ever-so-gently into the night wind.

The jeep works its slow way up the fire trail, dislodging fair-sized rocks to fall soundlessly into the valley far below. I almost can't stifle an urge to throw all my weight to the side of the jeep farthest from the abyss, like the crew of a sailboat in high seas.

"Yep, Hank," Dick says. "More than one jeep has found its way to the bottom of this valley."

Then he laughs, because he knows as well as I do how many miles we've logged on these trails, and he knows why I'm preoccupied just a little bit. It is October 1978, over three years since

205

Dick raced down these very same trails, with the tires of his jeep fighting for purchase on the rocky surface. Three years since I'd died and been reborn on an August afternoon on the side of a mountain.

And now I'd come back.

I'd been to the mountains once before, but never to the side of old Ajax, the *place* itself.

But now I'd come back.

I have my reasons, both large and small. I need to see it again, to make the picture come into focus in my mind's eye. I need to feel the rocks underneath my feet and breathe the cold wind from the other side of the Continental Divide. And somehow, on an even deeper level, I have to remind myself that the mountain is still here, unchanging. Mostly, I just need to be *here*.

The trail is little used and hard to find, and the going is tough even for a jeep. The switchbacks are so steep that we have to work our way around them, inches at a time. It's a long way back down to the Big Hole.

At the base of Ajax there's the remains of the old mining camp, which consists of one cabin still standing and two or three collapsed. The wood is old and weathered and looks more like it grew up out of the mountain rather than was put there by the hand of man. The cabin that is still on its feet has a rotting old mattress, a pantry with food that you'd eat if you were desperate enough, and a huge four-burner, cast-iron-and-enamel, woodburning stove. "Whoever carried that stove up the mountain deserves a lot of posthumous credit," I think wryly. It'd take a helicopter or somebody with a great sense of humor and a dangerously low regard for his own life to try to cart that thing up these trails today.

All over the cabin are carved the initials of those poor souls who've taken a night's refuge here. Taken what they needed and left what they could spare, then moved on into unrecorded oblivion. From two winters ago, a short note left by somebody hiking through the mountains and caught in a blizzard. "Provision running low and have to try and make town God bless." In another few years the writing on the note will fade, and finally even the paper itself will be gone.

But even then the cabin won't be empty.

We leave the jeep parked next to the cabin and head up the skirts of Ajax. At first the going is easy. The land is rising ever so slowly alongside the clear mountain lake. The snows are late this year, and, amazingly enough, it's still springtime in the high country. The flowers have only just recently pushed aside last year's snow to spend their brief time in the sun, and the air is alive with the feeling of growing.

But the lake is ice cold and the color of a finely blued gun. The ice itself is never far from the lake.

We're still far enough below the timberline that we have to work our way through the underbrush and tall evergreens, following the shore of the lake until we reach the base of the mountain proper.

It is a jumble of rocks, as if a cosmic dumptruck had unloaded a million tons of granite in sizes from large boulder to small pebble. One huge rock chute, all the way to the top thousands of feet above. We pause before starting up.

"I don't suppose I have to warn you to be careful," Dick says. I laugh, and we start climbing.

The climb is strenuous, but not hard. I am in good shape, and I feel my muscles work in unison, expanding and contracting as I move up the mountain. I feel the drag of the holster on my belt, and the Ruger .44 Magnum resting there. I can almost smell the combination of leather and gun oil. I am breathing a little heavily, and in the chill air of the early afternoon it feels wonderful. I am alive, and I feel it in every pore.

My thoughts drift like the wind blowing out of Idaho, to the snow bridge that has capped Ajax since time immemorial, past the nimble grace of my friend Dick Willey as he climbs, on down the mountain, to the cabin where my wife, Becky, and our unborn child wait, sitting in front of a roaring fire and watching their dreams in the dancing coals. There are snatches of songs here, waiting to be caught, blowing on the edge of the wind like my random thoughts. Every song ever sung here plays on the wind, as well as a million songs just waiting to be born. They're the songs of the elk, thanking the mountains for a late snow that leaves them in the plush meadows. They're the songs of the bear, grumpily preparing himself for his winter's sleep. They're the songs of the mountain goats, visible as tiny specks moving through the high mountain clearings, singing their songs to the hard granite cliffs and knowing they belong here more surely than any man.

They all flow around me in an infinite symphony, tantalizingly just beyond reach.

My mind drifts to my own song, and it too echoes through these valleys.

> . . . Way out where the blues will never find me
> Oh, I'm going to Montana to rest my soul . . .

I don't think the blues are trying to find me now, or, rather, I'm not trying so hard to find them. I think I left the blues on the side of this mountain, along with a lot of other things.

> I wish that special someone was going along.
> But she don't love me anymore, so I'll be gone . . .

We reach the top of old Ajax, the point where the rocks gave way and the chute shifted to settle itself. Above us looms the snow field, an icy crown on the top of Ajax. Below us is the lake, looking so close that for a second I wonder why I didn't just dive into it.

And then it comes back, in slow motion, and I see a tiny, limp dummy tumbling and falling, soaring and sliding down the mountain. I feel the dummy struggle to survive, and feel the hopelessness when it realizes that it can't. I see the boulders coming up like an express train, and I hear the *sound* again, as I've heard so many times since. I see the dummy raise his hands to his face, and I feel his shock, again.

I shiver as the cold wind blows out of Idaho and sends ripples skating across the lake.

It really happened, I think. It really happened.

Then I feel the cool peace of the mountains touch me, a gift from the Being who chose to make the mountains in the beginning. And I offer a prayer of thanks, and the prayer is accepted.

We start down, Dick and I, and we are very careful. We pass the spot where I came to rest, and the gray boulders are stained in deep rust-brown. We continue down, and I realize, once again, that sometimes it takes the mountains to give a man perspective, to show him that there are things bigger than his exalted heights.

My thoughts roam back down the mountain to Becky, and as they do I can feel the traces of a song blowing on the afternoon wind.

I smile, and work my way down.

Behind me, just out of my reach, I can almost hear guitars.

26

Closing

I've been off the road now for three months, and I'm going to stay off the road until my child is born. Lots of people—J. R. included—have pointed out that it has cost me a fortune to lay off the road for that long. Mostly, I just shrug it off, because I've gotten to know Becky better than I've ever known any woman. What that alone means can't be measured in terms of dollars and cents.

I decided to go off the road in September 1978, and there were a lot of reasons. I'd been on the road solid since September 1976, after the fall. By solid, I mean around 300 dates a year—again. Texas one night; Colorado the next; then California; then Maine; then Virginia; then home for two days.

The road is a funny mistress and it's terribly easy to get seduced. You can sink back in that world, in the back of a bus or the front of an airplane, and the real world will become just a haze in your mind. Believe me, I know how easy it is.

But the toll is high, like the proverbial old deal of selling one's soul to the Devil. You can have the road for a few years, but sooner or later The Man is going to come collect his soul.

I'm also not as strong as I used to be, something that I find hard to accept, and something that I'm constantly trying to do something about. After about a year and a half of heavy touring, the dizzy spells came on, and they scared me down to the roots of my being. I'd stand there on stage and feel everything start moving around in circles. Then I couldn't breathe, and I'd choke and gasp until it seemed like I was going to pass out. Then I'd drift back to normal.

I didn't waste any time going to the doctor. He ran a lot of tests and, not surprisingly, came to the conclusion that I was working too much. Rest, he said.

But sometimes I'm a stubborn cuss, and I'd been placed back on this world to play, and play I was going to do. I put in six more months, with the dizzy spells getting worse. At my first stop in New York City in a long time, I made three out of four shows. For the fourth, I couldn't breathe. I was going numb. I was scared. When I got back to Alabama, I headed to Panama City for a little rest, and I still couldn't shake the dizziness and numbness. Becky and I cut our mini-vacation short and headed to Nashville and the hospital. The results were the same.

Rest, they said.

I canceled my dates for the rest of the year, and Becky and I headed back to Alabama.

The only dates I kept were the ones with Waylon, because, in all honesty, those were the best dates I'd had in a long time. Waylon's fans are young people, and they're interested in what I have to tell them with my music. I'm still getting standing ovations.

Sticking to my own music, though, is awfully tough, because the pressure to "go back" is always strong. I've seen half the audience get up and walk out in disgust halfway through the show, and the other half stay on their feet screaming for more long after I've done my second encore. The ones who are screaming are the ones who keep me going.

See, country music audiences are still tricky animals. They're fiercely loyal—to a fault, I'd say. They'll stay with you come hell

212

or high water. They'll buy your records if your last hit song was in 1949. But the one thing they can't or won't tolerate is change. A country audience looks on an artist changing as a personal betrayal. For me, with my last name, the feelings of betrayal go even deeper.

Maybe I should compromise, I don't know. More than one person has suggested it, including J. R. Do your daddy's songs in your daddy's way, then go on and do your own music, too, they tell me. Well, I do play a couple of his songs, but I've got to play them *my* way. If I fail, the failure is mine, not the fault of some packaging operation for misreading the public.

You can package an act to fit the public taste and have a guaranteed hit. Just look around—in country music last year one major record company spent a rumored five *million* dollars to convert a country queen into a disco pop star. She has hit pop records and releases special disco versions of her songs. But is that so different from what Mother tried to do with me? Isn't that just another way of denying your own talent and having a convenient excuse handy when you fail? I'm not looking for a safety net. I would rather throw the dice and let them fall.

But I'm not going to lie to you about that, either. I was born with a safety net—Daddy's royalties, which come whether I'm a star or not. It seems like every year someone records one of Daddy's songs and has a hit with it—Linda Ronstadt doing "I Can't Help It If I'm Still in Love With You," or Michael Murphey and John Denver doing "Mansion on the Hill." Next year I'm going to be getting exactly half of what I got this year. After twenty-six years, Mother's gambit failed, and the courts ruled that, despite her insistence to the contrary, there was *another* Mrs. Hank Williams—Billie Jean Jones—and she had a right to share in the royalties. That the decision took twenty-six years is an indication of how knotted up it actually was. The legality of the "wedding," performed not once, but twice, on stage in Louisiana, was always in question, and Mother had always insisted that Hank was ready to come back to her, and that they'd already made plans to be married again.

Water under the bridge, I suppose. But the safety net is still there, and that's why I won't compromise on my music. Success or failure, the responsibility is mine and mine alone.

That much the mountain gave me: the ability to cut through the bullshit and deal directly with the heart of the matter. The mountain was a double-edged sword: One side of me now tends to be overly cautious, but the other demands that I throw caution to the winds, because I might be dead tomorrow. As long as I maintain a balance between the two, I can slice through the trivia like a warm knife through butter.

That tends to make people uncomfortable. You'd be amazed how much of your life is cluttered with worthless trivia. The new girl at the office isn't working out; the office politics are running against you; I've lost this or lost that, and what *am* I going to do? Throw that stuff out of your mind, and it seems an awful lot clearer.

My mind is clear.

And I have my religion, my God. I'm not going to go up there on stage and try to sell it, either, although there's a huge market just waiting. Sometimes I feel a certain amount of . . . well, pity, for people—performers in particular—who have to wear their religion on their sleeve. I wonder if they really know what it's like, having their life given back to them.

Sometimes I think of my religion the way a stubborn mule might think of a farmer. A mule's attention span is equal to roughly twice the length of the board you hit him with. The Lord had to hit me with a pretty big stick, but He surely got my attention.

Now I do the best I can to live my life the best way I know how, which sounds hopelessly trite, I know. I'm pretty lucky in more ways then one, and there's things I want to do and places I want to see. I've even gotten over the usual artist's crutch—I'm happy and I've got people who love me. I'm still searching for my father, and that's a search I don't think I'll ever finish. The historian in me is fascinated by that time in the South's history, and the son in me is proud of the part Daddy had in shaping it. But the self-pity is gone—just the opposite, in fact. Seems like every time I find a new song about Daddy or the South during that period, every time I get on stage and sing it, I learn a little more about myself. That alone makes the search worth continuing.

And I'll tell you one thing for certain: I'm not going to die a broke, drunk country singer. I've really made my mind up on that point. Even if I'm not a singer, I'm not going to die a broke, drunk *anything*. Period.

I will not do it. No matter what my family name is.

Amen.

INDEX

219